The Secret
Eater

Ros Jackson

Cover art: Laura Hollingsworth
Editing: Anna Genoese

www.rosjackson.co.uk

PRAISE FOR THE SECRET EATER

"This novella is filled with interesting characters, a unique world where demons exist right under humans' noses, and ... adventure" —The Bookish Daydreamer

"Jackson's writing style is fun and easy to devour." —Jaclyn Canada, JC's Book Haven

"This short tale is fast paced and full of fun characters with their own unique attitudes about how to be a demon!" —Tome Tender

"Normally I don't want to root for the success and wellbeing of demons, but Kenssie was such a relatable character." —Kate Policani, Compulsively Writing Reviews

"Well written story that kept me hooked." —Krystal Clear Book Reviews

"Kenssie is hilarious ... She's a great combination of naive, snarky, and mischievous." —Quintessentially Bookish

"...written in a delightfully engaging fashion ... a very fine debut" —Little Ebook Reviews

"... a fun little read full of mystery, magic, mayhem and some intriguing demons" —Literary Sweet

"You will read it in one sitting because it's near impossible to put down!" —Lose Time Reading

"The Secret Eater left me hungry for more" —Literary R&R

"The way Ros Jackson has portrayed the demons and hybrids of her world makes them seem a perfect complement to our fears, insecurities, greed and anger." —Humanity's Darker Side

DEDICATION

To David and Rowan.

CONTENTS

ACKNOWLEDGMENTS

I owe the following people my gratitude for helping to make this novella better than I could have made it alone:

Anna Genoese, for editing it with an eagle eye and catching all of those commas I somehow managed to miss.

Laura Hollingsworth, for turning my rambling description of Kenssie into a funky cover.

My first readers Kate Deaves and Elizabeth Le Ster.

I'm grateful to all of my family for their patience, encouragement and helpful advice. Thanks to David for being awesome, and reading every single word aloud. Above and beyond.

I'd also like to thank Andy Remic and Nancy Holzner, whose comments on my last manuscript have helped me immensely with this one.

CHAPTER 1

"I can see you, demon. What do you want?"

Kenssie turned round from the bookshelf she'd been examining — herbals mostly, interspersed with the latest from Hugh and Nigella, but with some very interesting forbidden spellbooks sprinkled in. The woman was staring straight at her. Talking to her. And that could mean only one thing: she was a powerful witch.

"So you can hear me. Get off my things."

Kenssie narrowed her eyes in a way she hoped was intimidating. She straightened her shoulders. Stared the witch directly in her deep brown, too-seeing eyes, and prepared to show her exactly why demons were feared. The witch stared back, unflinching.

"Come on," the mortal demanded.

Kenssie focused, feeling her head swirl with the whispers of stolen thoughts, and an electric surge as her power coalesced in the air around her. It hummed with energy, ionising the air and making the carpet under her feet crackle with static. Soon, the woman's life would be hers. Kenssie would have every moment from her birth onward.

The power grew, swirling furiously like a wormhole tornado, opening a psychic portal between demon and victim that would flood her with power.

"Stop that. It's annoying."

Kenssie was outraged. How dare this mortal speak to her like this! She focused her mind for a devastating pull, enough to rip ordinary mortals all the way down to insanity. She bared her teeth and felt the air grow thick, whilst the smell of copper and ozone filled her nose. Then she unleashed the magic.

And . . . nothing. Not so much as an embarrassing faux pas at a dinner party. Not even her name. Either the witch had just experienced an attack of amnesia that had wiped out her entire life history from memory, or she was extraordinarily resilient, even for a witch.

Kenssie's shoulders slumped. At times like this, she was grateful for her thick, concrete-grey skin. The heat had risen to her face, but it would never show. It was time to scrape some dignity from the situation.

"You can see me because I wish you to, mortal."

She stepped forwards out of the corner of the room. Her attempt at a cool glide was hampered by a tangle of scart leads she hadn't noticed, and she tripped and fell forwards. She would have landed on her face, but the witch reached out and grabbed her shoulders. They hung for a split-second in an uncomfortable embrace. Then Kenssie righted herself and stepped back as though the mortal's touch burned her.

She scowled. They stared at each other once more, witch to demon. Kenssie couldn't read her at all.

"You're welcome," said the witch.

"Er, sorry. Thank you," Kenssie said, dropping the act. This was humiliating. Not only could she not hear a single one of the woman's thoughts, she was making a fool of herself into the bargain.

"You should tidy that lot up, it's a hazard."

"I'll bear that in mind next time I'm expecting demonic burglars."

"You must be a very powerful witch."

The witch looked at her strangely, head cocked to the side so her long, dark hair fell loose like velvet curtains.

"Not really. I'm only a level one."

Kenssie didn't know what that stood for, but it was so like the humans to assign grades to each other for everything. Even so, level one didn't sound very good.

"Still, I can foresee great things for you," Kenssie said.

"Whatever." The witch shrugged. "Just tell me who sent you."

Kenssie grimaced at the implication. Nobody had sent her. She was her own demon!

"I have no master," she lied.

"So why are you here?"

There was still a chance to get out of this with some dignity intact. If this ever got back to Rakmanon . . . she didn't want to think about the consequences. The witch was scowling at her, pink lips pursed, and Kenssie realised she'd better think of something fast. Focus. She'd just used up her last reserves of power, and if the witch turned on her, she could put Kenssie on her back for a month.

She reached behind her and pulled a thick book off the shelf.

"I came for this. This is demonic knowledge, not meant for mortals, and I'm taking it back."

The witch's scowl loosened and curled into a wry half-smile. "Sure, take it. I always suspected as much."

Kenssie looked down at the tome in her hand. She was holding Nigella Express.

***

She walked through the centre of Lincoln, taking comfort in the crowd. Here, at least, her superiority was unquestioned - these people couldn't see her. She was tempted to stand on the bridge and moon passers-by to prove that point. But you could never know when a witch was going to walk past, so she refrained. Besides, it was childish.

She was still reeling because she hadn't been able to read the witch's mind. The woman had worn a long black dress, criss-crossed with purple cord at the front, like being a witch was a lifestyle choice. She probably owned a black cat and a willow broom. How had she blocked Kenssie's power? It was as disconcerting as forgetting how to walk or do up buttons.

What was really troubling, though, was that this wasn't the first time something similar had happened. She'd noticed it several times before, when she'd failed to read someone who should have been easy. She'd put it down to fatigue, bad luck, too much poison - but there was no denying it any more. Her powers were waning.

She felt a light psychic tug. It was Rakmanon's call, gentle and firm, like a pull on a leash. He never called twice; he never had to. She'd been hoping to return to her place in the country, but now she turned back towards the train station.

In London, she fought her way through crowds to his office. She hated the tube. Crushed together like cattle, in that environment, invisibility was a liability as much as a benefit. It was faster than hitching a ride in a cab; usually she would take her car, with its deeply tinted windows, but she'd left that in Cambridge.

Rakmanon's offices were on the fifth floor of a shiny new building. The interior was all gleaming chrome railings and touchpad technology, a glass temple to modernity and clean lines. Kenssie thought it had no soul.

"You took your time," Rakmanon said as she entered his office.

"We don't all have wings," she replied, bowing her head automatically.

The sight of Rakmanon still took her breath away, even after all these years. He was nearly eight feet tall, and muscular like a bull, with two tightly curling horns to match. His deep red skin shaded to black at the tips of his wings, which he had folded back tidily. He rarely smiled, but she knew he had a set of pointed white fangs that would make a jeweller salivate. She loved the shape of his jaw, so firm and well-developed. His crystalline eyes fascinated her the most, so piercing and inscrutable. Rakmanon was perfect.

He leant back in his chair, regarding her indulgently with one eyebrow cocked higher than the other.

"There's going to be a convocation. You'll accompany me of course."

"A general convocation?"

That would mean all the demons in the country; those were rare, perhaps only once a century - and often dangerous, or so she'd heard, but usually exciting. She'd only been to one, but she'd been a baby at the time and had no memory of it.

"No, only a London one. But there'll be some nobs there, so I need to put on a good show. You know what to do."

Kenssie nodded. Like most demons, Rakmanon fed on human emotions, but only certain strong feelings nourished him.

"And make sure your own powers are topped up, too," he said. "I can't have you making a fool of me."

"Er, about that," she said.

She wondered how much of the morning's humiliation she should spill. Rakmanon looked at her impassively, waiting. She felt hot as his eyes bored through her. She didn't want to say anything, but there was something compulsive about his gaze, something about his pit-black eyes that made her want to tread coals to keep them on her. She couldn't help herself.

"My own powers aren't working properly. I'm having trouble with the simplest things."

"Be specific."

Rakmanon said this with a tone of command, and she had no choice but to obey.

"I went to a witch's house to leaf through her books. She saw me. I tried to read her mind, and couldn't."

"How hard did you try?"

"Hard. I'm losing my powers, Master."

"It's not the first time, is it?"

She shook her head, feeling wretched. She hated to look so weak, especially in front of the one demon she needed to impress more than anyone else.

"It won't do," he said.

Her cheeks boiled. If there was one time she wished she could use her power of invisibility, it was right here, right now. But this was Rakmanon, and she'd never be able to hide from him. She was losing her powers, and she had to do something about it otherwise she'd never rise in his esteem, and her dream of him seeing her as an equal one day would be so much dust.

"I'm going to take it to the council!" she announced.

"Ha!"

He slapped his hand on the table, a sturdy steel and mahogany affair that he still managed to make wobble like cardboard. "They'll eat you for lunch."

She scowled. She might be a young demoness, but she had to stand up for herself.

"They have to listen. What's happening to me could affect all of us. It's serious! They've got to help me."

"You've been listening to too many humans. They don't owe you anything."

Rakmanon's deep rumble of a response made her realise how much she was squeaking. She took a breath.

"I'm going to ask them anyway."

He sighed, and the air filled with the scent of smoky musk. Her nostrils flared in pleasure, and for a moment she forgot what she was going to say.

"You'll be humiliating yourself," he said.

"So will you forbid me to approach them?"

His cheek twitched slightly. "No. I'm warning you not to go. But you have free will in this matter."

"What else can I do?"

"Find another way to get your powers back."

"But there's no other way I know of. I don't even know what's draining them."

"They're not my powers. Not my problem. Now, go torment the mortals for me. Have fun, but not enough to make you sick."

He swivelled to the side, and she felt an immediate mental relaxation. It was a dismissal; the leash had been slackened. She backed out of the room and rode down the steely lift. Fun? She was far too miserable for such a thing.

CHAPTER 2

The council inhabited a grand old building with lead-paned neo-Gothic windows and architectural flourishes that made the stonework seem alive. It was a big enough setup to necessitate witch thralls working the commercial front to guard the place from nosy humans. This year they were posing as Solar Investments, a green energy firm with grey branding and a website that would never get past the "coming soon" stage.

Kenssie drove down the long driveway in one of Rakmanon's Mercs, its windows tinted illegally dark. She sat on top of a shop dummy, so humans wouldn't freak out when they saw a driverless car. One of these days, someone would sell a car capable of driving itself - until then, she'd have to put up with plastic digging into her backside. Stupid humans and their stupid bony legs.

She parked at the front of the building and locked the car with a beep. The witch standing at the door stared straight ahead. He was a black-eyed young man (or so he appeared; it was hard to judge age with these hybrids) with bodybuilder muscles and shoulder-length hair. He looked bored. She trod softly across the paving, pleased that he wasn't following her with his eyes. Good. At least she had the power to fool some witches. She paused as she passed him and considered rearranging his clothing, but he turned and looked her straight in the eye, exposing rows of sharply pointed conical teeth behind his smile. She hurried in.

He was a half-breed, with enough of the blood to show demon traits. Such creatures always made her uncomfortable.

The lobby was dark and hushed, its walls hung with reproduction Bosch paintings over paisley wallpaper. Busts of Roman emperors lined one wall. A deep mahogany desk dominated the back wall, framing the kind of rich purple winged chair beloved of retirement homes. It was as though someone was going for gravitas but only got as far as gravy.

Another witch sat in this chair, her bouffant Marmite-black curly hair not quite concealing two vestigial stumps sprouting from her head. Kenssie determined to ignore her, and marched directly to the door leading to the council chambers. It was locked. She rattled the door, assuming it was stiff, but it wouldn't give.

"You can't go in there." The witch's voice was smooth and mellow like a coffee advert.

"Open the door! I need to see the council."

The witch looked at her with a tight expression. If she had had horn-rimmed spectacles, Kenssie was sure she'd be peering over them.

"You can't go in without a permit. Council rules."

Kenssie leaned across the desk and fixed the witch with her best malevolent stare.

"So give me one."

"Sure," the witch said brightly, rifling in a desk drawer. She brought out a thick sheaf of papers and slapped them down on the desk.

"That's the permit?"

"That's the application form for a permit."

Kenssie picked up the papers, which were heavy and stiff. She thumbed through to the back: 114 pages.

"You expect me to write you a novel? Just let me through."

"Council rules."

"The council can shove their rules."

Kenssie bared her teeth at the witch, who didn't flinch a millimetre.

"I'll be sure to mention you said that."

Kenssie got up and shook the handle again, then gave the door a shunt for good measure. It did not budge. She thought about yelling at the council beyond, but decided that would be too undignified.

"I'm sorry, but it won't open without a permit, and I can't get you one without a form. That's just the way it is."

The witch's tone had turned sympathetic, and she held out a pen for Kenssie to use.

"You'd best make a start."

Kenssie snatched the writing implement, a blue biro, and huffily took a seat at the side of the room.

"Answers must be entered in black ink," the form admonished.

The narrow plastic seat wobbled as she adjusted her weight and looked at the booklet. Name. Age. Master and/or thrall name(s) and age(s). That seemed easy enough. Then she got to page two.

Demon number. Birth mother. Birth father. Their demon numbers. Their percentage of demonic blood, and so on through five generations of family tree. She didn't know this. Who did?

A few pages farther on:

Have you ever been seen by the council and had a ruling go against you? Have you ever been banished by this or any other council?

She ticked "no" and turned the page.

Have you ever been seen by a mortal?

Umm . . .

Are you intellectually subnormal? Tick yes if someone had to explain those words to you.

And then a kicker.

Have you ever eaten, or been tempted to eat, mortal food?

She had. The experience always left her feeling sick and dirty, but every once in a while, she succumbed to curiosity and hunger. It was a secret vice she didn't like to talk about. She ticked "no."

How many times in the last century have you had to poop? Did anyone have to help you with this?

She couldn't believe she was reading this. She threw the form at the witch in disgust. It caught the air and flapped uselessly to the ground like a misguided seagull.

"What is this?" Kenssie demanded.

"It's the questions they need to ask," the witch said with maddening calm. "I don't make the rules."

"Have you read this stuff? It's perverse. It's humiliating. It's the form from Hell."

"Kinda suitable, don't you think?"

Kenssie looked around at the Bosch paintings, and the shelf behind the witch stacked with Dante and Aleister Crowley.

"Is this your idea of a joke?"

The woman was leaning back, sweat beading on her upper lip, her eyes wide.

"Oh, shit, she's worked it out."

Kenssie heard this, but the sound wasn't coming from the witch's lips. It was a secret straight from her head. Kenssie focused her power. Her head thrummed. This is what she should have done all along, she realised, but she hadn't wanted to waste any of her reserves. Now she pushed herself, and probed into the witch's mind. Little by little, the barriers came down.

"Don't think of the permit. Don't think of it. Black pudding and custard. Black pudding and custard. Black pudding and custard. Hollowed-out Inferno. Black pudding and -"

Kenssie jumped up on the desk and lunged for the copy of Dante's Inferno. The book was indeed hollow, and out fell a blue crystal key on a chain. She grabbed for it, expecting a tussle, but the witch wasn't even going to offer that much resistance.

"Don't go in," she warned instead. "Everyone regrets it."

But Kenssie could hear her true thoughts now, as if a tap had been opened. The witch, Permilia, would get into trouble with her master, and that was all she was thinking of. She couldn't care less about what would happen to Kenssie, good or bad - just her own sorry mortal self.

Kenssie took a deep swallow of Permilia's secrets. Then she put the key in the lock. It turned with a satisfying click and she stepped through into a bright, long corridor which led on to a single door at the end. The council chamber.

The air in the corridor was stifling. She felt as though she wasn't so much walking through the hot, stuffy atmosphere as wading through it. She pushed on, sensitive to a kind of psychic resistance that was telling her to turn back. This only made her more determined to go through with this. What did they think she was, human? Only mortals would give in to such a shoddy psychic tug. It was insulting.

She flung the door open and emerged into the bottom of an enclosed amphitheatre, where she stood on waxy floorboards oiled to a treacherous gloss. High above her a wood-panelled gallery circled the room, where all the council sat in judgement. It was disconcertingly quiet, so even her footsteps sounded too loud to her.

"Kensssssssssie."

The speaker was a deep green Krakenite demon, undulating with tentacles. His face was an octopus-like globe that tapered down to a fringe of smaller tentacles where a human male might have a beard. The demon's mouth was in there somewhere. He had thicker, arm-like appendages, like squid tentacles - about eight of these. The creature wore a tartan check scarf around what passed for its neck, and he stared at Kenssie with outsize liquid black eyes.

"It's Kenssie. Only two esses."

This was Haames. She'd met him before; she knew that, out of sight behind the panel, he walked on two legs that ended in thick cloven hooves, and on his back he had two vestigial wings that were thick like flippers and about the size of Kenssie's hands. Haames claimed to be tens of thousands of years old, dating from the time the first demons entered the sea to evolve into Krakenites. Kenssie had her doubts.

An assortment of other demons were arranged to his left and right. They looked down at her with eyes beady and black, slitted, gelatinous as lime jelly or glowing like orange coals. Her eyes were drawn to a black demon, jet from head to toe, who towered a head over the others, even whilst seated. His horns curled up like Danish pastries on either side of his head, and his expression was closed.

"The answer is no," Haames boomed.

"Wait a minute, I haven't even asked my question yet!" Kenssie protested.

"We know what you want."

"In that case, my question is: will you refuse to give me back my powers?"

Haames waved his arms around in jerky little motions. She thought he was trying to summon his powers, or perhaps he was having a fit. It took her a while to realise he was actually laughing.

"Very cute," he said.

"What makes you think you have the right to demand anything of us?"

The voice came from his left, from a yellow-skinned demoness wearing a grey gown that made her look like a sickly hornet. Her name was Fiuru, and Kenssie knew her as an anger-feeder.

Kenssie put her hands on her hips and gritted her teeth.

"I have as much right as any demon! My rights have been violated.

Someone is leaching me, I'm sure of it. You must help me."

"We will be the judges of that," Haames said evenly.

"We don't have to do anything about this," Fiuru objected. "Why should we?"

"What else are you here for?" Kenssie asked.

The black demon held his hand up for calm. "We will test her."

The speaker's voice was deep and crackling. The room filled with static and all eyes turned to him. Haames waved his tentacles at the black demon, and a hush spread through the gallery.

"Good idea, Salamhat," Haames said.

"Test me for what?"

Haames stilled his tentacles and fixed his round ramekin eyes on her. "We only help deserving demons of our own kind. It's a test of demonity."

Kenssie bristled. She rubbed a hand over one of her horns, then brought her hand down and made a fist. She bared pointed teeth, all too aware of her wingless back and soft feet. These were cosmetic differences, though; they meant nothing. She'd show them.

"How do we know you had any powers of your own in the first place?" Fiuru cawed.

The gallery turned to Kenssie and bared their teeth right back at her.

"Bring it!" Kenssie said.

Hisses and jeers rose like the spray of the ocean. Haames slapped his appendages for quiet, and got it.

"Bring in Inkado."

Kenssie fought to suppress a shudder. Inkado was an ancient name, one given to demons tens or even hundreds of thousands of years in the past. She didn't know any Inkado, but she'd heard the name in legends and guessed he was old and correspondingly powerful.

"Inkado? Are you sure?"

The speaker was Suninn, a short, brown demoness with a scar on her forehead that looked a bit like a tick.

Haames nodded. Suninn got up, shaking her head, and left to summon this Inkado. Several minutes of thumb-twiddling later, a concealed door on the lower part of the courtroom was opened, in a space that had looked like no more than a part of the panelling. The witch, Permilia, opened it with the help of a male witch. The male had no visible signs of his hybrid nature.

They wheeled in a large white cot covered in lace and frills. From inside it came a rhythmic snoring, like an industrial machine.

The demon baby was nestled in soft pillows, like a beating heart in a bed of meringue. It was plump and red, its two tiny horns already curling up over its shiny bald head. Little black eyes burned like coals over a snub nose, and two chips of white teeth were growing through at the front. Tiny but perfectly formed claws grasped the blanket, and the sight of it made something stir inside Kenssie. She decided it was probably nausea.

"What's this all about?" Kenssie asked the gallery.

"This is Inkado," Haames said.

"This? It's a baby!"

"You pass the observation test," Fiuru said.

"What do you want me to do, babysit it?"

Haames's voice resonated like a movie intro. "You must defeat him in a contest of enthralment."

"But I'm enthralled to Rakmanon. I can't have thralls of my own!"

Fiuru sneered. "I'm sure he won't mind."

"It will be temporary," Haames said. "The rules are simple. You must make the witch give you this rock before he gives it to Inkado. You must remain behind the white line, and you may not touch the witch."

Haames threw down a stone, which the hornless witch caught and held up to show around the room. Meanwhile Permilia withdrew, locking the door with a click.

Kenssie frowned. "This witch is already a thrall."

"Indeed," Haames said. "In a moment, I will release him from his bond, and that could get messy. Are you ready?"

"Ready."

"Ga-aaa-bah!" Inkado said.

Haames raised a tentacle, then brought it down.

"Begin!" he said.

The witch let out a piercing scream. Eyes wild, he darted around the room and started scratching at the panelling. He was looking for the exits, which were concealed in the rest of the panels, so it wasn't apparent where the doors were. He avoided her and the child.

"Quickly now," Fiuru chided. "He'll get away."

Kenssie focused her will on him. It wasn't easy because he kept moving, and he was ducking and dodging as though he was avoiding invisible fireballs.

"Let me go!" he yelled. "You've no right, you -"

She tried to suck out his secrets. She'd never enthralled anyone before. She'd never been given the chance like this, and she didn't know how to do it.

The witch was vehement. "Thirty years of making tea for witches and pushing pens. I had plans!"

She felt something. Snatches of secrets: a hidden stash of digestives, a pet marmoset kept without a license, a wardrobe full of women's clothes. Nothing substantial, but it took the edge off her hunger and made her feel stronger. Yes, she could do this. The man had stopped running around and now he wore a more pacified expression. She was draining him, so it was time to begin the enthralment process.

Then he took a step towards Inkado.

"No, not that way, this way," she said.

The witch took another step. Titters from the peanut gallery made her look up. As she broke eye contact, the witch took two more paces, his hand rubbing the stone and his expression moving from calm to a kind of open, beatific stupidity. She swore under her breath and kept her eyes on him.

"Come to me," she said. "Come to me, or I'll tell everyone about the shoes."

The witch hesitated, but his smile remained the same. He inched back her way. She plucked his name out of his head. Stewart, but his friends called him Wiz. Or they used to, back when he had human friends, back when he was allowed that freedom.

Come to me. Be my thrall.

Stewart took another step her way. Was this really how it was done? Could it be this easy? She couldn't help but think of Rakmanon, and what he must have done to make her his thrall. But that was different, their relationship was special. Wasn't it? She felt a warm glow when she thought of him, but she made herself push it down. Right now she had to concentrate.

Inkado let out a frustrated wail, and thrashed his arms about. Stewart turned his head to the baby and took three steps towards it before Kenssie could stop him. She teetered forwards, catching herself before she stepped over the line. Above her, one of the demons sniggered.

The witch was getting away. Damn it, she couldn't lose this contest! It was humiliating enough that she struggled.

Come to me. Come on.

Stewart turned to face her again. He stepped backwards.

Not that way, this way. Come to me!

She held his gaze, digging nails into her palm as she exercised her powers. She was fuming with herself. Why wasn't she stronger? Her temples throbbed as she exerted her will on the man, and she felt bone-weary. This had better be worth it.

Suddenly, Inkado let out a high-pitched, shrieking laugh. Momentarily distracted, Kenssie lost eye contact with Stewart. It was enough. He padded over to the cot and placed the stone gently in Inkado's tiny hands, gazing at the infant demon like he was a confectionery god.

Raucous laughter erupted all around.

"Beaten by a baby!" Fiuru laughed.

"I let him win!" Kenssie said.

"Aw, look at his beautiful eyes and his cutesy-wootsy toes," Suninn said.

"Are you sure he hasn't enthralled you as well?" Haames said, shaking.

This was no test. They'd set out to see if she would dance for them, with no intention of ever letting her win. Well, she'd show them. She'd get even.

With a giggle, Inkado threw the stone out of his cot, and the room erupted in applause as Stewart ran to fetch it. Kenssie ran out into the corridor and slammed the door behind her.

CHAPTER 3

They bred like vermin and took over the place, but humans always made good eating. Their range of emotions made them the most flavoursome of all the beasts, and, boy, was she ready for some comfort food.

A slight mental tug reminded her that Rakmanon was hungry, too. She slipped into the multi-occupancy office block adjacent to his HQ. Slack-jawed office zombies shuffled from water cooler to grey desks, studiously avoiding making eye contact with each other. Dead-eyed exhaustion and premature greying seemed to be the office fashion on the bottom floor, where a firm selling cheap ink had its administrative headquarters. They were mined out down here, Kenssie decided.

She sprung upstairs, taking the worn, carpeted steps two at a time and following a woman unseen into the Ladies. The law firm Parkin, Cheese and Slaughter was a smorgasbord of juicy secrets, made especially delicious thanks to the lawyers' absurdly high opinions of themselves. She had a lot to thank the British higher education system for. They must have gone to law school specifically to learn how to look down on everyone else.

The woman emerged from the cubicle and went to wash her hands, checking her face for smeared makeup and any new lines. She was forty-something, so she had a few. She wore a knee-length black skirt that flared slightly. Perfect.

Kenssie snuck up behind her and picked up a tiny pebble from a plant pot. With a practiced hand, she threw it at the window; as the lawyer woman turned her head at the noise, Kenssie tucked the loose skirt into the woman's underpants. Shaking her head, the woman dried off her hands and checked her nose one more time. Then she left, with Kenssie hard on her tail.

Computers weren't Kenssie's favourite toy, but they had their good points - the CC field in the email programme, the web history filled with porn, the screensaver that went on the blink when was meant to cover up a game of Angry Birds. She slipped into an unoccupied seat and started typing. Passwords were no barrier to her when she could steal secrets from people's heads. Her fingers flew over the keyboard. Sometimes it was the revelation of a secret shame that did the trick, but other times it was the simple application of the delete key - crude but effective. She spent half an hour flitting from desk to desk, making sure messages got misdirected and bad habits exposed.

When she heard a howl of dismay from a nearby cubicle, she knew she'd struck pay dirt.

"My work here is done," she whispered.

She exited the building and was disturbed to find a witch waiting for her. It was Permilia, the one from the council, the one with the awful form. She wore a thick beanie hat to cover her horns.

"What the heck are you doing here?" Kenssie demanded.

The witch smiled, exposing rounded, even teeth. "I believe we may have got off on the wrong foot. I'm Permilia."

The witch extended a hand. Kenssie ignored it. With her pale, ivory skin and heart-shaped face, Permilia was almost pretty - for a human.

"Like I care. Get out of my way."

"We want the same thing."

"Do we? I don't remember 'as much humiliation as possible' being on my Christmas list."

"I tried to warn you."

Kenssie pushed past her briskly. Permilia followed, rushing to keep up.

"Look, I don't have long. I'm in trouble for being here as it is."

"Good."

The witch got exasperated. "Will you just listen to me? There's a book. A grimoire. The council is using it against you."

Kenssie turned to examine Permilia's face. The witch almost

barrelled into her. She was a thrall of the council, no more, so what was their game? More humiliation? It seemed likely. There was no reason for them to give up on her if they thought she was good sport. Well, she'd learned her lesson and she wasn't going to bite. Nosiree.

"I know how you can steal it."

Now she was sure they were listening in. One of them would just pluck this conversation right out of Permilia's head.

"As if I would do such a thing. I'd report you, but I suspect they already know what you're up to."

"Don't be so sure. We have more in common than you think. When you get bored of being powerless, call me."

The witch handed her a black card unadorned by illustrations, with her contact details on it.

"I'm hardly that, witch."

***

Kenssie listened to the soothing whirr of the air conditioner and the quiet swish of the lift as it opened. It was a relief to get away from all those pesky halfbreeds. So when she spotted that the desk outside Rakmanon's office was occupied by a woman in a long purple dress, her face fell. The woman looked up from a laptop she was furiously typing on, flicking back long, dark strands of hair. It was the witch from Lincoln.

"You!" they both said.

Kenssie scowled at her and marched into her master's office.

"You can't go in -" the witch began.

"What's she doing here?" Kenssie demanded.

Rakmanon looked up from sawing the head off a My Little Pony to regard her with a smug smile.

"Ah, Kenssie. Here at last. I'd ask you how it went with the council, but I'm not one to rub in salt and gloat. Oh, wait. Tell me in detail how it went with the council."

"You already know."

He nodded in acknowledgement. How did he find out so quickly, when he didn't like to use phones? She guessed it was a higher demon thing. She motioned to the witch outside.

"Yes, that's Jenny. I see you've met."

"What's she doing here?"

Rakmanon gave her the look he'd give a slow-witted infant.

"She works here. She's my new thrall. The convocation, remember?"

Kenssie's heart, already in her lower abdomen, dropped to somewhere around her sneakers. A thrall could be here for decades. She'd have to put up with the obnoxious woman's hippy ideas about witchcraft, and her sneering knowledge of Kenssie's true place in the demonic hierarchy. It'd be a constant reminder of her fading powers. And, worse, she wouldn't have her master to herself any more.

"Is something wrong?" Rakmanon asked gently.

She coughed and shook her head. "It's nothing important."

If she didn't know any better, she'd think he was trying to feed off her, like he would from a mortal. But that was impossible.

Her master stood and walked towards the window. Although this was a new building, it wasn't one of those safety-locked windows that only opened half an inch, but a wide, floor-length one that opened onto a ledge without a sniff of a safety rail. Outside, London buzzed and hummed, the grinding engine of the human meat machine. He beckoned her to him.

"You know you'll always be my favourite," he said.

Kenssie allowed herself a smile, and nodded. He ruined the moment by chuckling at her, then enclosed her in his thick red arm and opened the window. She clung tightly to him, realising what was about to come. This was what being a thrall was all about.

The wind was fresh; five storeys up, it enhanced her vertigo. Rakmanon pushed off with a powerful thrust and spread his wings wide, beating them furiously. For a sickening beat, they fell . . . and then they were up in the air, soaring over the city. She clung to his torso, her fingers sticky with sweat, her heart racing due to the flight and his proximity. The smell of him and the warmth of his body sent thrills through her, and there was no hiding it. She looked up to see his fangs flashing with the delight of being airborne, his face lit up.

The air whipped across her face, cool and invigorating, whilst Rakmanon was growing warm with exertion. She clung on tight and gasped as he took them higher. His wings beat fast and rhythmically. An air ambulance helicopter flew by on their left, close enough for Kenssie to make out the pilot's face, oblivious to the pair of them. Rakmanon sped up a little as it passed them, and she squeezed her arms tighter around him and bit her lip.

They crossed the Thames and flew towards Surrey, where the city gave way to leafier suburbs. Traffic was heavy, but it didn't matter - this close to Rakmanon she was enveloped in his psychic aura, and invisible to all mortal eyes.

"We're here," he announced.

Too soon.

He tucked his wings and they dived towards a large walled garden. She let out a squeal like a kid on a fairground ride, full of exhilaration. Then they were down, Rakmanon spreading his wings like a parachute so they landed softly on the lawn, stepping until the momentum was spent. He released her from his arms.

"You can let go now."

She peeled her hands reluctantly from around his back. His taut torso was a delicious memory.

The garden was surrounded by high brick walls and contained a good acre of private land, mostly made up of tightly-clipped lawn, bordered with shrubs and mature yew and oak. There was a large Georgian house to the south, and this was where they headed.

"Nice pad," Kenssie said.

The place looked deserted, and she wondered whether they'd got the right location. Not that she would ever question her master of course, but . . .

Then she saw a grey shape flitting through the bushes, and she knew they had the correct venue. The house loomed over them, a four-storey mansion of period stateliness begging for someone to make a costume drama in it. Her low heels dug into the lawn, and she wished she'd had the chance to change into something nicer. She hated turning up to a party in the same blue cords and frilly white blouse she'd had on all day. It was so typical of Rakmanon not to notice these things. He wore a sharp black suit cut to allow his wings free movement, but even if he'd been entirely naked, he wouldn't have batted an eyelid.

Clothes were a modern weakness, he'd say.

She went to use the heavy brass bell, but Rakmanon strode past and right inside. The interior was just as Pride and Prejudice as the exterior: someone had gone to a lot of trouble to have it gleaming with polished wood and period décor. A wide, sweeping staircase curved up from the lobby like a long red tongue.

"Whose place is this?" Kenssie whispered.

A female voice called out, seemingly from nowhere, "Ah, Rakmanon!"

Fiuru hovered above them, her yellow wings spread out to their fullest extent. She floated down so softly Kenssie figured she had to be using magic . . . or strings. She was dressed in an elegant pale green gown with matching five-inch heels, great snub-toed things adapted especially for the cloven of hoof. They looked uncomfortable. Fiuru topped it all off with gobs of jet inlaid in a wide gold necklace, and a matching belt.

"Fiuru, always a pleasure," Rakmanon said.

Kenssie knew he didn't mean it.

"I see you brought your whole entourage. Let me see if I can find space for her."

"I brought one of them," Rakmanon said.

"Oh, and not the other?" Fiuru said, her voice full of mock concern. She was trying to imply he was weak because he chose not to have too many minions, but she was wrong.

"It's not the number, it's the quality," Kenssie said.

Fiuru looked down her nose at Kenssie and made a moue of distaste, regarding the younger demon rather like a talking dog. She clapped her hands. Seven small, grey demons flitted out of the doors and assembled at her command. Some of them had tails - but, like Kenssie, none had wings. They seemed to hold themselves in crouched positions, as though their lowly status was gradually turning them into hunchbacked Igors.

"Refresh our guests," Fiuru said. "Perhaps get this thrall a nice cup of tea."

Kenssie suppressed a hiss.

The grey minions led them off into a side room, and Fiuru excused herself to greet another newly-arrived guest.

"Remind me why we're here again?" she asked Rakmanon.

He beamed a thousand-watt smile. "You'll see. She'll be eating bread and butter by midnight."

The thought gave Kenssie the queerest feeling. Proper demons didn't eat human food, only half-bloods, so it was a grave insult. She'd dared herself to eat it before, as an experiment. It left her feeling heavy for about a month afterwards. She didn't like to think about bread and butter.

One of the grey thralls handed her a glass of water. She thanked him, and sniffed it tentatively. It wasn't that she was worried about poison; such a thing would only affect her minimally anyway. It was that she wouldn't put it past Fiuru to give them human pop as a deliberate slight. But it smelt clear, and when she flicked her tongue in, the water tasted just like water.

She tried to make conversation with the thrall.

"So, what's your name?"

He shook his head. In response to her puzzled look, he motioned to his throat, saying something in sign language.

"He has no voice," Rakmanon supplied.

Kenssie looked closer. "Did you have your tongue cut out?"

The thrall shook his head and signed something else.

"She made him un-evolve it," Rakmanon translated. "It was the only way the change would be permanent."

Kenssie looked at the uniform faces of Fiuru's thralls, their identical heights and their air of obsequiousness. She looked across at Rakmanon and shuddered. Evolution within one lifetime was something demons could do, but it was often fatal and fraught with risks. Fiuru was a cold demon indeed if she demanded it of her thralls on a whim.

There was the swooshing chop of blades as a helicopter arrived in the garden. It was big, black, lumpy, and insectile, with two round bulges above the cockpit. It touched down and disgorged a squad of demons who scattered to form two rows. A large bull demon emerged and walked down the centre. It was all very military.

Rakmanon sucked in his breath.

"Who's that?" Kenssie asked.

"Veishti."

He uttered the name like an ancient curse, with the whiff of bad blood in the air.

Veishti's skin was glassy and white, like a translucent reptilian egg. He stood seven feet tall, his bone-white horns curved so they almost met in the middle. He wore a sleeveless leather coat that brushed the floor, slit for his wings, which he had tucked in. His arms, stark white against his black clothing, stood out broad and muscular, and he seemed to have lots of metal jewellery on his lower arms. As he approached, she saw it wasn't jewellery at all, but piercings, threading through his skin like he'd knitted himself out of iron.

She had been feeling underdressed before, but now she wished she'd worn Kevlar underpants and a katana. She looked to her side, hoping to gauge Rakmanon's reaction to this display, but he was already out of the door, moving to intercept the new arrival. She raced after him, praying he wouldn't make a fool out of himself.

Rakmanon and Veishti met on the patio, and the sight of them gave Kenssie goose bumps. A static crackle arced through the air.

"Rakmanon, so good to see you. I was afraid you wouldn't make it."

Veishti managed to make his words mean the opposite of what he said.

"Likewise, Veishti. It's been too long."

Rakmanon's sarcasm was delivered with more cheer and a cheeky smile. Point one to her master: he was the better actor.

Veishti turned a greedy eye on her. "I see you've brought me a tasty gift."

She couldn't suppress a shudder. He reminded her of a shark, one with the skin of a jellyfish. Disgusting.

"And I see you've brought me many," Rakmanon countered.

Fiuru sauntered up. "Now, now. I know you're impatient for the main event, but that comes later. There's lots of other things to do first. Come, Veishti, I don't believe I've shown you my dungeon yet."

"Of course, Fiuru. Lead the way. I'll see you later, Rakmanon, if you still have the stomach for it."

"Count on it," Rakmanon said.

"What was that all about?" Kenssie whispered as they walked away.

Rakmanon turned to her; he looked inscrutable. "Nothing to worry about. Trust me."

Then he reached out and ran his hand down from the nape of her neck to her back. She shivered, but this time it wasn't from fear. He leaned in close, so that she could smell burnt toffee as he whispered in her ear.

"You're broadcasting. Try not to think of sea creatures. He's more eel than shark, believe me."

He winked, and she blushed at the reminder he could read her so well.

Two hours later, the convocation was buzzing with all manner of demons and their thralls. The loud music was a mix of screeching industrial metal and grandiose strings. Some of the younger demons were trying to out-dance each other - or perhaps they were fighting. It was hard to tell the difference. The lawn was alive with firefly lights glowing red, green, and blue. They swarmed around and followed everyone who didn't bat them away.

In a corner, a group of six demons were sprawled around a shrubbery, half-naked and in fits of giggles. They were inhaling Uninhibitor, a potion strong enough to kill mortals with a single drop. They offered her the steaming bowl but she shook her head. The effects would only last half an hour at most, but she wanted her head clear all evening.

"Come on, don't be such a stick in the mud," called a fat green demon lying on the grass. "What have you got to hide?"

The demon's name was Defoe, but everyone called him Greeny, and he was the thrall of a pity demon. Last week, his master had forced him to disguise himself as a mortal and sell really bad artwork in aid of a trip to Hull to visit his two brothers having chemotherapy. Kenssie got all of this from standing nearby; she didn't have to make the effort to pull it out of him.

"Um, I'll pass," she said.

"Spoilsport," said Greeny.

She pushed through the crowd. Not everyone here was a demon - some witch minions scurried around; some let their hair down and danced with abandon. The air tasted of their emotions, a thick sludge of wild release and pent-up anger: the feelings of slaves.

He's going to cut me up into tiny pieces.

Kenssie heard this in the mind of a passing witch in a miniskirt and spike heels. She wondered which demon had threatened this, but the witch moved on. It was odd. The place was full of so much raw emotion, she seemed to be able to pick up on anything, even from other demons.

I'm going to lose my home.

My master's going to freak when he sees my duck tattoo. Too funny!

I'm an artist. A sculptor of emotions. I can do this. I'm an artist. I can make a dog my thrall.

That latter was the thought of a short demon with stub-like horns.

"What would be the point?" Kenssie asked. "Dogs do what you tell them to anyway."

The demon jumped back as if stung. "Don't do that. It's rude to look into other demons' heads."

Kenssie shrugged. "It wasn't on purpose. You're broadcasting."

The demon scowled and backed away from her. She felt a powerful mental tug coming from the centre of the grounds. She ran to it, past sweaty bodies jumping themselves into a frenzy.

The music stopped. Since she'd arrived, they'd set up a sound system with a small stage in the middle of the garden. Lights fell on Fiuru, who stood atop it. She'd changed her clothes; now she wore a vast shiny yellow ball gown trimmed with black ribbons. It was gorgeous, and Kenssie felt a pang of envy eat her up. She'd been trying to think of Fiuru as a crusty old hag, but there was no denying the figure she cut now was more like Snow White's better-looking older sister than a crone.

She pushed through the crowd until she found Rakmanon, and was relieved to find he wasn't transfixed by Fiuru.

"Welcome to the South London Convocation," Fiuru announced, her voice amplified through the speakers. "I hope you've all been enjoying yourselves."

The crowd cheered and whooped.

"In a moment, we'll come to the event you've all been waiting for, whether you've been dreading it or drooling over it."

At this, she looked over at Veishti, who was next to the stage with a line of his thralls behind him. Rakmanon's face tightened.

"But first," Fiuru continued, "I have an announcement. I wanted to gather you all here one last time, and I thank you all for making the journey. But after this year, you won't be seeing me again, not in this manner. Because this year . . . I will be evolving!"

There were gasps around the wide lawn. Higher demons rarely evolved themselves, perhaps only once every four or five thousand years, and only if they were brave and powerful. It was one of the few ways a demon could actually die, and it took a lot of strength to ensure it could be done safely. How could Fiuru afford it? And what was she planning to become?

Fiuru broke the awed silence. "I bet you're all wondering how I could possibly improve on this form. Well, you'll have to wait and see! Now, for the event you've all been anticipating: the enthrallment contests. And, to borrow a phrase from the mortals, it's a real David and Goliath one to kick us off. Let me welcome onto the podium . . .

Veishti!"

There was a roar of support from his thralls. Kenssie thought it sounded forced. Veishti swaggered up with his grim death's-head face and thumbs tucked into his belt. He waved to the onlookers like a prize fighter.

"And, opposing him . . . Rakmanon!"

Kenssie whooped and hollered, making enough noise for a small army.

"Go Rak, go Rak!" she yelled, doing a little dance.

However she was the only one making any noise at all and all the eyes on her were pitying. Why couldn't they have at least brought Jenny? It was embarrassing.

Rakmanon walked up and gave Fiuru a nod. He didn't look at her or the crowd at all.

It happened so fast. One second they were at a lawn party, the next the ground opened up like a vast chasm. The rumble was momentarily deafening. Everyone standing in the centre fell in, and she scrabbled to the side to avoid joining them. The hole widened. Screams echoed up from the sides, and those who fell in disappeared into an inky blackness that seemed to go right to the core of the Earth. Soil from the sides of the crater fell on top of them, burying their cries.

Another crack opened up in the ground, splitting the soil in a thick finger aiming straight for a point beneath her feet, as if it were just for her. It opened under her before she could escape and she fell, grabbing at the soil. Dirt encrusted her fingernails. She snatched at a root and came to a precarious stop on a ledge so narrow only her toes had purchase. The ground shook. The soil between her fingers was too moist and loose, and her nostrils filled with the scent of earthy decay and sulphur.

A wave of heat belched from the bowels of the Earth beneath her. She looked down, and instantly regretted it. The blackness had been replaced by a malevolent orange glow. Lava.

Being a demon pretty much meant being indestructible, but there were limits to everything. The lava would destroy her.

She looked up again; the surface, and the safety of the ground, was a good twenty metres up. Had she really fallen that far? She could barely make out the relief of the sides in the darkness. How was she going to climb out? At times like these, she really wished she had wings.

"Rakmanon! Rakmanon!"

There was no sign of him. Above her, the noise of demons had receded, and below there was no sound at all. No screaming, because all of those who had fallen had died.

The root she was holding shook and crumbled. She lurched backwards, and clung to the side with the tips of her fingers. What was a root doing this far below ground anyway? She panted. Sweat slicked her hands. There was no time to think, she had to climb. She heard a belch like the bubbling of a porridge pot - the thick liquid was rising. She hauled herself up, hand over hand. Her eyes stung with sweat or tears or sulphur, she couldn't tell.

Then there was movement behind her, and something big streaked up. The wind from its wings almost knocked her down and it passed its lizardine bulk so close she could almost touch it. A dragon. And not a cute "Puff the Magic" one either. This one was all scales and teeth and T-rex ancestry, long and thin and vicious. It flew over the lip of the chasm; from the screams, she realised some of the people up there were still alive. They wouldn't be for long.

She climbed, though the effort strained her limbs. She was shaking. One false step and she'd fall. A clump of soil broke free and showered over her when she grabbed the side. Damn. She had to be careful where she put her weight. But there was no time. She could feel heat rising beneath her. She scrambled for a handhold, and missed again. The she found purchase, and hauled herself up again. And again.

A spine-shaking scream rang out. She looked up, and a long forked tongue whipped out above her. The coal-bright eyes of the monster looked over the rim. At her.

"Wait a minute, a dragon? In London? Veishti, you sonova -"

She took a breath, and smelt the earth and sulphur. The dragon snuffled and spat out blood, and a drop of it landed wetly on her face. The heat was still rising, and she had come no closer to escaping the pit in Fiuru's lawn.

Kenssie had a feeling, though. She'd better be right about this. A sick shiver crawled up her chest as she closed her eyes and pushed off from the side of the hole, letting out a small cry but managing to stifle it. Down, down . . . into the hot lava abyss.

She landed softly on dry, worn grass, and rose to find herself surrounded by a wide circle of demons and witches. There was no chasm in the lawn, no dragon. Veishti was staring at her angrily. She folded her arms, planted her feet, and gave him the evil eye. He was a fear demon, but he wouldn't enthral her. She knew his secret.

Rakmanon caught her eye and gave her a wink. That's my girl.

Veishti's thralls were still crouched all around, posed as though clinging to a cliff face, wide-eyed, with glassy expressions of terror. Veishti hadn't won her over, but he had an iron grip on his existing thralls and quite a few of the unaffiliated witches who were spectating showed signs of being in the grip of his illusion.

Rakmanon's expression was as unreadable as ever. He turned to the DJ.

"Hit it."

He moved to the centre of the small stage, where the spotlight hit him in shades of sweetie bag pinks and yellows. He raised his arms as though poised to perform a powerful spell. What did he have up his sleeves? Great big fluffy white sleeves, Kenssie noted, over slightly over-tight gold spandex trousers, flaring in deep inverted Vs. When did he find the time to get changed? He looked like a seventies throwback.

The music built slowly. Kenssie recognised the opening chords of the Bowie's "Let's Dance." Rakmanon started to move his hips from side to side. What spell was he trying to pull off? The music got louder, and he shuffled about, waving his arms and moving his feet half-heartedly and out of time. He was looking into the middle distance with a glazed, pained expression on his face, deliberately not meeting anyone's eye. A few bars in, he wiggled his hips suggestively, although the main thing it suggested was he had back trouble and maybe the start of arthritis.

Kenssie buried her head in her hands. This was Rakmanon's special attack? Veishti's fear illusion had dragons, volcanoes, and screaming mayhem. Although it hadn't taken her in, it had at least been a good show. To counter that, Rakmanon had . . . dad dancing? She wanted to crawl back into that magma pit for the shame of it.

Around the grounds the tittering grew. He moved on to "You Make Me Feel Like Dancing," then "Stayin' Alive," and then he bald headbanged to "The Final Countdown." Even his air guitar was off key.

Kenssie wanted to die.

She was mesmerised.

CHAPTER 4

"That went well."

"What? Are you insane?"

They were back in Rakmanon's office the next day, where he was reclining like he'd run a marathon. The frilly white shirt was gone, replaced by a neon Hawaiian number that hurt her eyes.

"In case you hadn't noticed, I nearly fell into a pit of lava, came close to getting swallowed by a dragon, and had to endure your dancing. We're no better off than we were yesterday!"

"On the contrary. Yesterday, Veishti thought he could have you. Now he knows he doesn't have that power."

"I came this near to being the thrall of a fear demon! And look at you, you're so depleted you had to take a taxi home."

Rakmanon hadn't done gloating. "Did you see the way he was looking at me? I nearly made Veishti my thrall."

Kenssie hadn't. She'd been too astonished to notice anyone else.

"He probably thought you'd lost your mind, like everyone else."

"Enough!"

Kenssie felt a pulse of energy as Rakmanon exerted his will on her, and she staggered back towards the door. It felt like being tickled by a school of fish - not brutal, but not altogether pleasant either.

"Get out there and humiliate me some mortals," he ordered.

On her way out, Kenssie nodded to Jenny. The witch waved back, which put Kenssie in an even blacker mood. So the powers she'd regained at the convocation had only been temporary - a result, perhaps, of the charged atmosphere. Now, the dust was settled and she was back to her underpowered self. Worse, she had an ache in her midsection she couldn't quite place, and her head felt fuzzy. Was this what the mortals called a hangover? Impossible.

***

Kenssie staggered out of the television studio, her legs buckling underneath her. She was shaking like a jackhammer. It was six-thirty and the late rush hour traffic was buzzing past. She emerged into a still-bright day, wishing darkness would fall, or at least some heavy smog.

Invisibility was a demonic trait that seemed to work like magic, but, in fact, followed logical rules. It worked on mirrors, video cameras, humans, and other base animals, but not on most demons, and it was more than a mere psychic trick. If it hadn't been, their secret world would have been discovered years ago, as soon as photography became widespread. Demons became invisible by exerting a power over their own bodies and the objects around them, but they also possessed varying degrees of special sight to see through this field. However, this power came at a cost.

Kenssie looked around the narrow side street. It was clear but for an old woman at the far end lugging shopping bags home, thankfully not looking in the demon's direction. Kenssie clutched her sides and doubled over, breathless. The street wouldn't stay so quiet, and she had to get away. She needed to hide, but the effort was wearing her out.

In the wardrobe of the dressing room of one of the presenters, she had chuckled to herself as she snipped the seams of outfits. The presenter was a blonde chirpmeister due to do a series of live interviews. When she came in talking through her daily checklist Kenssie dodged past and stood stock-still in the corner of the room. There was no doubt the presenter was human - she aged at a mortal rate. Kenssie had seen it from the woman's TV appearances over the years. So when the woman turned, jumped, and yelled, "Get out of here you psycho freak!" Kenssie had bolted.

That had been two minutes ago. She looked at her body, and willed it transparent. The thought set off an acute ache in the back of her skull, and the shaking increased. It was bad. Worse than bad, in a place so full of security cameras and film equipment. She pressed against the wall; she could hear a commotion in the building, and the sound of running feet. Her first instinct was to run. But if she did that, she'd deplete her reserves of energy, making it impossible to hide herself. So she stood still on wobbly legs, breathing and trying to focus.

She didn't want to be the demon who gave the game away to mortals. She couldn't be that person. Cthulhu's gloves, this was humiliating.

"Would it be a good time to renew my offer?"

Kenssie jerked her head around. She hadn't even seen Permilia creep up. The witch stood there with the same look of irritating smugness she'd had the first time they'd met.

"What the -"

"You didn't see me, did you?" Permilia asked.

Kenssie straightened her back, suppressing a wince. "I was looking the other way. Why are you stalking me?"

"Get in my car. We need to talk, but not here. By the look of things, I'm in the nick of time."

Kenssie scowled and folded her arms. But people were coming down the stairs towards the studio exit. Permilia made a meaningful glance in their direction, then back to Kenssie. She knew she was trapped. Her shoulders slumped and she relented.

"Okay."

Permilia didn't hang around. She grabbed Kenssie's arm and steered her round the corner into the back of a waiting BMW with deeply tinted windows. Permilia got in the driving seat whilst Kenssie climbed through the gap and took the front seat. The witch drove confidently away, keeping within the speed limit. It was the kind of driving no-one would remark on. The TV people were clattering about outside as they left, loudly proclaiming the strangeness of what the presenter said she'd seen, and speculating about stress and coke habits.

"You look like Patrick Swayze in Ghost," Permilia said. "What gives?"

It was a good question, but she couldn't answer it. Moreover, she didn't want to tell this busybody anything, so she didn't.

"Come on," Permilia said. "I just rescued you. Do you want me to dump you back out on the street, or are you going to tell me something? Were you trying to be seen?"

Kenssie rankled at the threat, but she realised she had no choice. She couldn't call on Rakmanon's help in this state.

"No, I wasn't."

"More's the pity," Permilia said.

"Huh?"

"I was hoping you had a bit of rebellious spirit in you. A political statement or something."

Kenssie shook her head. "I don't know why it happened. An accident."

Permilia shot her a cynical look, then turned back to negotiate a junction. "Oh, I have a fair idea. You're weak after the convocation."

This surprised Kenssie. "You were there?"

"Not for long. I try to avoid those things if at all possible. But I heard all about it at work today. Your boss, well, he's got the council's attention all right."

Permilia's lip quirked up.

Kenssie sank into her seat. Rakmanon seemed to have everyone's attention. Why couldn't he be more boring?

"What's that, fed up with your master? I told you we weren't so different."

Kenssie didn't like the way the conversation was going.

"Why are you here?"

"The grimoire. Something's come up."

Permilia drove on with her lips tucked under her teeth, as though she didn't trust herself to say another word.

"Out with it. You came all this way across town to fetch me, might as well spill the juice."

Permilia glanced across, seeing something with her witch eyes that Kenssie couldn't decipher.

"You're in no state to do anything about it. You're shaking with fatigue."

Kenssie breathed in and tried to still her legs. "Am not."

But she was.

"Tell me something: do you have an ache about here -" Permilia gestured at her stomach. "And trouble concentrating?"

"I'm sharp as a rack. A Taser. A thing."

"Been finding it hard to use your powers lately?"

She shook her head.

"Tch. You're a rotten liar. And do you find your clothes looser than usual?"

"What are you, Doctor Demon? How do you know all this?"

"I thought so. Listen, wait in the car. I won't be five minutes, don't touch anything."

Permilia pulled over and stretched a fat black beanie over her head. She hurried into a corner shop with yellowing apples on display near the door, and sauce-stained polystyrene on display on the pavement outside. Kenssie watched her go in, thinking how awful it must be to have to disguise oneself for the mortal world all the time. She'd never cope; today was bad enough.

When she was safely inside the building, Kenssie transferred her attention to Permilia's car. She could tell so much about people by the objects they surrounded themselves with. It wouldn't be right to betray the trust of someone who had just rescued her, of course. But Kenssie wasn't all about right and wrong; she was a demon, and she might as well live up to the name.

The interior of the vehicle smelt slightly musty, and there were sticky patches on the dashboard and seats where drinks had spilt. The glove compartment looked tempting. She opened it and rifled through. A guidebook to Kenya, some pink leather driving gloves, another ugly, horn-covering hat. Not so much as an embarrassing old CD. There was nothing of interest in the pockets of the side doors, just car manuals. Then, behind the driving seat she found a brown leather handbag nestling in a bed of dust. Inside was a wallet with a wedge of notes, a driver's license that had to be fake – it gave her age as twenty-six and her name as Permilia Hopkins, and the photo was edited to make her look more human. There was also a notebook covered in neat, tiny handwriting.

"I thought I told you not to touch anything."

"Do you also tell the tide not to come in?"

Permilia got in and slammed the door. She had a warm package in her left hand and the smell of it hit the back of Kenssie's throat like an assault. The witch snatched the bag away and deposited this parcel in its place.

"There's nothing in there for you. This is what you need."

"I doubt it," Kenssie replied.

"I don't."

Kenssie unwrapped the white paper covering. A chicken tortilla wrap steamed within its folds like a malignant tumour in a clean white shirt. She covered it over as if the very sight could hurt her.

"I don't eat human food."

Permilia eyed her sceptically and put the car in gear.

"In case you hadn't noticed, I'm a demon," Kenssie continued. "Here, you have it."

Permilia waved it away. "I ate last week. And in case you hadn't noticed, you're showing all the classic signs of human hunger."

"Impossible. I'm a full-blood demon."

They sped past buildings in the suburbs, the grey city giving way to leafy civic pride. Permilia spared her a quick, disparaging glance.

"No wings. No tail. Human feet. Weak powers."

"I could eat you for breakfast on a good day, witch."

"Weak, compared with other demons."

"I'm not a hybrid!"

Permilia's lip curled in mockery. "You keep telling yourself that. Don't waste that sarnie, it cost me four quid."

The food was making her feel peculiar. Its chunks of white meat glistened with rich sauce the colour of saffron. Her mouth was growing moist. She glanced at Permilia, who glanced back with an expression of amused superiority. The aroma of the food curled into her nostrils and made her want to cram it in her mouth. She wanted to curl up in a dark cave and never talk to another witch or demon - but she wanted to take the wrap with her. Its tangy sauce and moist, succulent meat promised a sensual explosion of flavours and textures.

The witch was navigating a junction and her concentration was on the road.

"I guess it can't hurt my physiology. We should be open to new experiences."

She bit down. Flavours flooded her senses, making it hard to concentrate on anything Permilia was saying for a while. Tomato, spices, the fatty juice of bird flesh, and the soft chewy bread danced upon her tongue. Juices oozed on her fingers, sauce splashed her dress. Ugh. It would stain, and if Rakmanon called her, he'd know what she'd done. She was no good at this. The chicken filled her mouth with sweetness, but instead of her usual disgust at the sensations, it felt like a release, a craving. She finished the whole wrap and licked her fingers. Perhaps she'd acquired a taste for human food? Yuck. Yet one more guilty secret she needed to hide from her master.

"Tell anyone about this and I'll kill you."

Permilia laughed. "You say that as though human blood is a bad thing. Nothing shameful about being a hybrid."

They sped through traffic, the witch cursing when a blue van cut in front of them. Kenssie sank back into the soft leather seat, her limbs heavy. All that food had left her lethargic and she wanted to sleep for a week.

"You owe me big time," Permilia said.

Kenssie peeked open one eye. "Little time."

"This is twice I've rescued you. Three times, if you count undermining Veishti, which I do. You could have been the thrall of a fear demon."

"I didn't see you there."

"I fight him in my own ways. Never mind that - the point is that you have to help me."

"What's in it for me?"

"The source of the council's power, the grimoire. If you steal it, you can get your abilities back, and more. I'll tell you where you can find it and how to obtain it. But you have to do something for me first, and we haven't got much time."

Kenssie rubbed her eyes. "What's the rush?"

"Veishti's going to kill one of his thralls. Tonight or tomorrow, we think. He's got to be stopped."

This stirred vague memories of terrified, paranoid thralls. Looking into their minds was never pretty.

"Wait, wait. Relax. He's a fear demon, he thrives on this stuff. They're always threatening to hack someone or other up, but they never carry out their threats. Otherwise they'd have no thralls left."

Permilia shook her head angrily. "No! He means it! I haven't got time for you to doubt me. We've got to do something now."

Kenssie tried to soothe her. "I don't think that's how fear demons work. They're all illusion and no real bite."

Permilia's knuckles grew white on the wheel. She braked hard at a bend, and then accelerated out with a lead foot.

"No, you're wrong. Every once in a while, they have to carry out their threats. Otherwise everyone believes the same thing you do. Without belief, they grow weak, and Veishti's anything but weak."

"Why me? I'm not exactly cut out for going against Veishti."

"It's your fault! If you hadn't weakened him last night, he wouldn't need to build his power by terrifying his thralls."

This didn't make sense to Kenssie. "I thought you wanted him weaker?"

"I do. I just didn't expect him to pull this."

"Why are you so bothered? You're not one of his thralls."

Permilia swung a hard left and braked sharply in a driveway.

"No, but my son is."

CHAPTER 5

How do you tool up against a fear demon? Not with silver bullets and armour plating, that was for sure. All the late night vampire movie marathons were no use to her. Throwing popcorn would be about as effective.

Permilia rooted around noisily in her kitchen cupboard. She brought out several fat syringes, the kind a vet might inject a horse with.

"Liquid courage. Use it on yourself as a last resort."

"Alcohol?"

"Alcohol, foxglove, mandrake, hemlock, a bunch of other stuff. It's a cocktail of some of the strongest poisons. It's enough to kill a human, so it'll knock your mortal side out for a while so that Veishti can't feed off it."

"Feed? Off me?"

Permilia gave Kenssie a withering look. "How did you ever survive childhood? Yes, off you, Princess Precious. Why else have part-human thralls, if not to snack on?"

Kenssie felt her colour rise. Rakmanon would never do that to her, would he? Surely she'd know about it.

"Here," Permilia said.

The witch handed her a dozen syringes and she put them in her hip bag. It was time to go fight for thrall rights.

"What's your plan?" Kenssie asked.

"Go in. Don't get killed. Don't panic. Inject as many of his thralls as possible, then get them out of his range so he can't keep his hold over them."

She gulped, wondering what their chances were. She didn't like Veishti, she wanted to get back at the council for humiliating her, and someone had been stripping her powers. If she could stop him murdering his thralls, that was only right. But she wasn't sure she had it in her to defy a powerful higher demon.

"You look scared," Permilia said. "Don't be, it'll be fun."

"How do you work that out?"

"Because if it isn't, we'll both be chow."

***

She'd expected an inner-city crack house full of gun-toting gangsters, or a sweaty dungeon out in the wilds under a run-down Gothic pile. The City of London hadn't been the first place she'd thought of, but it made perfect sense. Before they got out of the BMW, Permilia sat and stared at her. She supposed the witch was mentally preparing herself, but the scrutiny went on too long.

"What?" Kenssie asked.

"Your colour is much better."

The concrete-grey, mottled skin on her hands looked the same as ever.

"I mean your lack of colour. You maybe can't see it, but you're like a ghost to me, and a very thin mist of one at that. My demon sight's pretty good, too. It must be the food."

The food in question still sat heavy in her stomach, but she had to admit she felt better for it. Her head was clear, her stomach wasn't clenching, and she'd stopped trembling as well. Damn Permilia for being right. Still, she didn't feel ready for this.

"Come on," Kenssie said. "Let's go get blancmange-face."

***

The streets swarmed with black-suited executives clutching smart phones in damp, white-knuckled hands. The air thrummed with worries. They marched into the stock exchange building with its bulbous sculpture in the foyer. Permilia's face was set in a fixed grin as she tried to avoid the humans walking into her. Witches weren't invisible, but they gave off an aura of "don't notice me" that allowed them to blend in.

Information scrolled by in acid-bright lettering on both sides of them. Prices up, prices down, and the whole lot shifting and wobbling like a storm-tossed sea. It was hard to imagine all of these decimal-point changes making or breaking anyone's fortunes. They made their way upstairs to the trading rooms. Kenssie's heart beat faster in anticipation, so she adopted Permilia's strategy of wearing a fixed grin and thinking of nice things. Puppies. Fat, juicy adulterers. Flying with Rakmanon.

Permilia motioned her to stop outside a large trading room, and they cautiously checked it out. Rows and rows of people sat at computers, looking for all the world like a typing pool. No glassy white horns. Kenssie allowed a smile of relief to climb up her face. However, there was a demon in the middle of the room, bent over a monitor a trader was working on and relaying text messages. Permilia pointed to him and then to herself.

Kenssie nodded. She spotted another demon at the far end, doing much the same job. Both of them had their backs turned. She took out a syringe and trod quickly and softly, hoping the demon wouldn't turn around. As she approached, she saw the trader at the desk had his head in his hands, as though he was napping. Fuelled by adrenaline, she leapt at the small, grey demon and plunged the syringe into his neck, pumping it all the way down.

He turned, his eyes full of fury, and backhanded her off him. She stepped back as he advanced on her. He pulled the syringe out and flung it aside.

"What have you done to me?"

Traders looked up in surprise at the disembodied voice, and she saw the one with his head in his hands wasn't asleep at all. His eyes were red-rimmed and puffy. Kenssie chewed her lip, wondering if the serum would render the demon visible. She hoped not.

"I'm saving you," she said.

The demon frowned and reached for her, his fist clutching the air. He made one shambling step forwards before his legs buckled and he fell to his knees.

His breath was ragged. "Saving? I couldn't live without Veishti. I'll kill you!"

She stepped further back, amused more than concerned by his threat. With his human side weakened, he didn't make any further moves. The anger on his face shaded into confusion. He looked around like he was waking up from a dream and he didn't know where he was.

The traders shrugged and turned back to their work. Kenssie figured they hadn't seen anything, they'd only heard voices. She gathered her power and drew from the trader who'd been crying.

Losses of three hundred and eighty-seven million. I hope no-one finds out.

It was an ordinary enough secret, not even that big for the city gamblers, but it strengthened her nonetheless. Turning, she spotted Permilia. She'd also succeeded in injecting her mark, another small grey demon. But they were wrestling. She ran to help as the people on the floor started to notice the noise behind them. Permilia was struggling, but before Kenssie could lend a hand, she headbutted her assailant square on the jaw and sprang to her feet.

Dusting herself off, Permilia glanced at Kenssie. "What? I had it under control."

They retreated warily.

"How long does it take to work?" Kenssie asked.

"It's already having an effect. The rest of them will be coming for us any minute. Veishti will have felt that."

She examined the demon on the floor. He wore the same confused look as the other one, and he was rapidly relaxing into a dopey stupor. A trader turned from his desk and looked at Permilia, who was dishevelled and panting. He raised an eyebrow.

"Delivering a message," she told him.

He turned back to his console, uninterested.

"We should get these people out of here," Kenssie suggested as they moved away. "Smash the fire alarm or something."

"Are you insane? He'll feast on their fear."

"He's doing that anyway, isn't he?"

Permilia shook her head. "We can't beat him by starting a panic."

But Kenssie doubted they could beat him at all. She kept this thought to herself. There was no sense in worrying Permilia. She glanced at the grey demons, both of them on their knees.

"Will they attack?"

Once again, Permilia shook her head. "Look at them - they're already shaking off his influence. While their human sides are knocked out, he can't feed from them."

"But only demons can be made thralls. Shouldn't they be more susceptible to his influence?"

"Don't ask me how it works, I just hope it really does. Heads up."

The witch pointed to a door at the far end of the room, where six demons marched through. Some of them were grey, whilst others were pink or brown. But all of them were small, horned, and intensely frightened. Their brows dipped with furious determination that distorted their faces. It was too much to expect any were afraid of the pair of them.

Kenssie palmed a couple of syringes. "Time for my ninja skills!"

Permilia eyed Kenssie sceptically, taking in her slight frame and the girlish, pink dress she'd chosen to wear that day.

"You can fight?"

"I heal instantly. That's almost the same thing."

The demons advanced, fanning out and moving round the central bank of desks. One of them climbed on top of these, pulling out cables and scattering papers as he progressed. Traders cursed when they lost their internet connection, then carried on with their work, oblivious.

Clocks ticked. People sipped coffee from cardboard cups and typed instructions. Kenssie ran to meet a grey demon, Permilia at her heels and then overtaking her. This one was female, and taller and thinner than the rest. Her smack sent Kenssie flying to the wall, clutching her jaw. But Permilia was fast and she came round the side of their adversary, injecting the demoness right in the neck. Kenssie struggled to her feet. Permilia was already tackling the next one, disregarding the demoness, even though she was about to brain the witch.

Kenssie pulled the demoness away and joined the fray again. Someone hit her about the face, and someone else elbowed her in the gut. She wasn't having fun.

Demons piled on to the two of them, kicking and punching. She was able to heal whatever they threw at her, but it still hurt and she didn't have the chance to use any more syringes. It was all she could do to stop them grabbing her bag and stomping the medicine underfoot.

"Get out of here," a pink-skinned male with short horns told them. "He'll order us to kill you."

He punctuated this by punching Permilia in the face.

Unlike Kenssie, Permilia wasn't healing rapidly and her face was a mass of growing welts.

"He'll kill you, Archie. I'm not leaving with you in his power."

Archie grabbed his mother by the shirt and gave her an anguished look. Then he slapped her.

He spoke through clenched teeth. "You have to. Go."

Kenssie and Permilia fell in a heap as blows rained down. More demons arrived and piled into the fray. Elbows, horns, feet, knees, all of them connecting with the softest parts of her body. Kenssie groaned. She couldn't see out.

Even if they wanted to run at this point, they couldn't. They were at the mercy of Veishti's thralls, and he was a killer. Blood ran down her cheek, actual blood. The grimoire had better be worth it.

She saw a flick of steel. Permilia let out an "Uhh!" and sagged. She'd been stabbed. Kenssie looked up at the crowding, angry faces of demons around her. She put her arms up to fend off their blows, realising it would be ineffective, and hoped they'd be merciful.

Then a chink of light opened up as one of the demons circling her was lifted up and away, a surprised look on her face. Another one gasped as the same happened to him. Kenssie wiped blood from her forehead and heard Permilia's gurgling breath beside her. Still alive, then.

Their saviour was the whey-faced demon she'd tackled earlier and stuck with a syringe. He looked lucid.

"Give me another of those syringes," he said, fists wheeling.

She picked herself up and scrabbled to pass one over.

"So, you're one of us now?"

"I'm free of Veishti's influence. I feel like death warmed up though."

He didn't look it, the way his arms were windmilling. He looped his right leg behind a demon and hooked him onto the floor in a textbook judo flip, sinking a syringe into the other's bicep as he went down. Meanwhile, the small grey demon Permilia had injected earlier had turned on his own group as well.

Kenssie ducked a kick coming from a brown demon, and scooted over to Permilia. The witch was lying on the floor with blood pooling out between her fingers, held over an abdominal wound. Kenssie's eyes widened.

"Not . . . as bad . . . as it looks."

Kenssie gulped. It was the wrong time to show fear, so she tried to make her face more neutral and nodded. Could Permilia die? She didn't know how quickly the witch could heal; she might be little better than a mortal at this sort of thing.

Then Permilia gasped and looked up. Kenssie turned, only to be met with a chair over the side of her head. The knock laid her flat out on the serviceable carpeting.

"Right. Enough is enough," she said.

The chair-wielder was Archie.

"Sorry, I had no choice," he said.

Kenssie screwed up her fists and picked herself up. So she was no ninja. She couldn't karate-kick to save her life. But she was damned if she would show fear. Veishti himself couldn't enthral her, so she wouldn't take this treatment from his minions.

"Time to take your medicine!"

She leapt at him and they locked in a grapple. He was stronger, but she was angrier. While they wrestled, she bore down on him psychically, sucking images from his mind like a fast-forwarded movie. Cookie jar misdemeanours. A horde of stuffed animals in a bomb shelter. A lab. A human lover from post-war Volgograd. An addiction to eating face cream.

She gorged.

His arms bulged with muscles, but he couldn't prise the syringe from her sweaty grip. They were at a stalemate. Under the acid glare of office lights and monitors, they fought on.

"Fight him," she urged. "He wants to kill you!"

"Never! It's an honour to serve, a sacrament! You know this."

She did. Looking at the fervour in his eyes, just for a second she thought of the pain she'd inflict when she broke that bond. She remembered Stewart.

It was enough hesitation. Archie took the opening and grabbed her syringe, tossing it behind him. She couldn't take her eyes off his snarling face as he advanced on her. She braced for impact. Then Archie's stance changed. He straightened, gasped in pain, then rocked forwards. Behind him, wielding an empty syringe and a smug expression, was Permilia.

The patch of floor where the witch had been was now occupied only by a stain soaking into the carpet like red wine.

"I thought you were dead," Kenssie said.

"Again with the underestimation. I should be insulted."

"Good job you're immune to criticism."

Archie fell to his knees. "Oh, God!"

His skin didn't look so pink and healthy any more, and he seemed about to throw up.

"Is he going to be all right?" Kenssie asked.

"Sure," Permilia said. "He's more demonic than he looks."

The witch didn't look overly concerned, although Kenssie thought that could be the resignation that came from blood loss. Around them, the tide had turned. Some demons had chased others out of the room and were continuing the fight elsewhere, but several were on the floor with dazed expressions and needles poking out of them.

Traders at computers were staring round-eyed at their work, fingers flying.

"Tin's down six!" cried one.

"Hawkins, you have to check the derivatives in Asia. They're bonkers!" another said urgently.

Men loosened their ties and panicked whispers spread round the room. She felt the tension roll off them.

"He's influencing them," Permilia said.

Kenssie saw sweat-soaked brows, exposed whites of eyes, hands gripping the edges of desks. She heard uneven heartbeats, and knew it was true.

"Can we take your son and the others and get out of his range?"

Permilia shook her head. "He's here."

The room seemed to shrink. Veishti was at the door, taller than she remembered, and closer already. She felt gripped by an urge to get away, to get as far from him as possible as soon as she could. Permilia turned and stepped away. Quick as light, Kenssie grabbed her arm and held her fast.

"Don't run. It's what he wants."

Permilia eased off. She was shaking, but she had more control of herself now.

"I'm alright. Let go of me!"

Veishti strode forwards slowly. Flashes of lava and dragons came back to Kenssie. She blinked them away, knowing they were unreal, but a thought itched at the back of her mind: he could make her believe anything he wanted, so he could kill her without touching her, making her do things to herself out of fear. Panic rose unbidden.

Beside her, the clacking of keyboards sounded like a train coming in.

"Mining stocks are down eighty percent!"

"Sell all our tech and buy gold!"

"Crude oil is down to two dollars, but I can't get hold of any. What's up with that?"

"What's going on? All my shares are down, and gold's right down, too. That never happens."

Their cries of alarm grew louder as traders noticed their fortunes sliding. In her head, Kenssie saw the faces of monsters getting clearer and more vivid. Her skin was spreading with an infection. Patches of healthy grey turned angry red and then rotten green as corruption crawled up her arms, bubbling and blistering. It was painful.

"The dollar's been devalued!"

This was accompanied by a fresh surge of agony as the disease attacked. She wanted to grab a knife and cut out the infected flesh before it had a chance to spread further.

"The Euro's collapsed! They're returning to old currencies!"

Kenssie threw up foul black liquid, oily and full of worms. She could taste the sharp vomit on her tongue, and feel the gritty creatures as they rolled around her mouth. It felt real. But it was an illusion, wasn't it? Now she wasn't so sure. She didn't know the extent of Veishti's powers.

His voice was the hammer of Big Ben. "I call them my reaping worms. You have no time. Cut them away, or they will consume you."

"They're not real."

"Oh, but they are. They're my special project. Don't you think I would have more than one power?"

Kenssie looked on horrified as her greening skin cracked, oozed and blackened, and juvenile versions of the worms emerged from her wounds. She didn't believe him, but Veishti was gaining power. Soon it wouldn't matter whether or not he was lying; she would be in his power. They all would.

Permilia was on her knees, wiping frantically at her arms with a grim look on her face. Most of the traders were in a blind panic, eyes wide and arms flailing. Then she spotted one of them, a young man with dyed white-blond hair and a moleskin jacket. His eyes were half-closed and his head was thrown back in a hearty laugh, like he'd won the lottery. What did he know that the others didn't?

She focused on him and pulled out his secrets. He had some, all right, but they were nothing special. He'd lost as much as everyone else in the room, shares wiped out and millions off his portfolio. But he didn't care. Why didn't he care?

Then Kenssie had it, and a grin spread over her face as she turned to Veishti. She leapt up and stood on a table at the side of the room, giving Veishti and everyone else a clear shot at her. She could see everyone there. Then she decloaked herself. For demons, this took an effort of will, like holding one's breath, because it was the suppression of an automatic reflex. It felt like a shiver passed through her whole body, leaving her feeling exposed but not cold, and a slight but tense pressure lodged at the very top of her head.

The effect of seeing a demon materialise on a table in the trading room was . . . not the surprise she was hoping for. A hush spread around the room. People noticed her, and went quiet as they pointed to her and gawped. Some of them didn't even turn at all, they were so absorbed in their own affairs. Then, gradually, they turned back to their workstations and continued panicking about their lives. They dismissed her.

Kenssie's mouth dropped open. "Stupid TV," she whispered.

She put her hands to her head and ran her fingers along her horns. Yes, still there. What would she give for a big, impressive pair of wings like Rakmanon's right now! She cleared her throat.

"MORTALS! BOW BEFORE ME, PUNY HUMANS!"

They looked around, and a few of them raised their eyebrows. That was better.

"ARE YOU ENJOYING MY SHOW?"

"Do you mind," a trader heckled. "We're a bit busy. Global financial meltdown, what?"

"Yes. Rather diabolical, isn't it?" Kenssie said.

They looked around at each other.

"Did you hack the computers?" asked a trader, whose bushy black eyebrows reminded her of caterpillars.

She looked at her feet and rocked, mock-bashful, back and forth. "I'm such a naughty girl."

This got a couple of giggles, but more shouts of annoyance.

"We've got work to do! Bugger off!" Caterpillar Brows yelled.

"Are you one of those protest groups?"

"Commie skanks! Get a proper job!"

Kenssie grinned, and looked at her arm. It was clearing up nicely. Permilia was standing now, a grin decorating her face.

"Oh, I'm not a protestor. From your point of view, I'm something much more interesting."

She winked out of their vision, counted silently to three, and let them see her again. The gasp of surprise went round the hall. Now she had them.

"I'm a representative of . . ."

She paused to think of a good name. Something cool and futuristic and not too pompous. She couldn't, so she went with the first thing that came to her head.

"Fearless Technologies. I hope you're ready to think of investing in us."

"You just wiped millions off the markets," said a blue-suited trader. "Are you insane?"

"A little. No, I jest. We're completely cuckoo."

Arms folded and brows furrowed.

"Okay, that was in bad taste. It's an illusion - you'll find the markets back to normal, and none of your recent transactions went through."

She hoped that was true. Murmurs of assent told her it mostly was.

Across the room, Veishti looked smaller than before, and further away. He was also out of control, sweating from the effort he'd expended. Yet these people had bounced back and accepted her explanation, no matter that it was absurd. They were resilient to fear and ready to believe the most optimistic thing because they wanted to. Traders around the room punched each other on the shoulders and grinned, and a few started laughing loudly. But Veishti wasn't giving up without a fight. They'd robbed him of his minions, who were now ranged around the room looking at him in his weakened state, not even running from him. He would not fight as they did, it wasn't his style. He turned on his heel and stormed out.

Permilia's son walked up to her, fists clenched in fury. "I can't believe you've exposed yourself like this! Mortals can't know!"

"Relax," Kenssie said through her teeth. "They think I'm dressed up."

She turned to the traders, who were shaking their heads and

shrugging their shoulders.

"Not listed anywhere," Blue Suit said.

"Never heard of Fearless," said the white-blonde one.

"What do they even make?" asked Caterpillar Brows.

She slid into the mind of Caterpillar Brows as easily as a knife through warm butter.

"Hey, you in the itchy fishnets!"

Caterpillar Brows looked at his colleagues.

"Yes, you!"

"I'm not wearing fishnets!"

His rapid colouring told another story.

"Would you like a demonstration of our neural-electric espionage technology? It really is advanced."

The trader shook his head.

"No? Too shy? Secrets too dirty? Can I have some volunteers please?"

CHAPTER 6

Rakmanon tapped his hand against a solid thigh, his scowl deepening. His eyes were hypnotic. Kenssie looked up from his office floor. His will kept her crouched there with a pounding pressure on the inside of her skull, which got worse if she tried to stretch above this invisible glass ceiling.

"I should dress you in motley and make you evolve a donkey head."

"He's your enemy. I thought you'd be pleased."

"Thinking's not your strong suit, is it, Kenssie? Because if you'd given it any thought, you'd realise I'm not ready to challenge Veishti outside of a convocation. He could easily have taken you as his thrall."

He'd changed his tune since yesterday.

"But he didn't."

"Shut up! I didn't say you could speak!"

She cowered on the floor. She'd rarely seen him so angry. Fury rolled off him in waves.

"You got away by the skin of your teeth. He'll be back. He has friends. And, thanks to you, the human cattle have seen us once again. That hasn't happened on such a scale in six hundred years."

She wanted to protest that every one of them had bought her story. Some of them literally: she had a wedge of cheques in her bag to prove it. But the power pushing her to the ground was also compelling her to show respect. Shame pulsed through her.

"You're a disgrace to demonkind. All this effort we put into balancing the humans' emotions, and you put it in jeopardy on a whim. You could have started a panic, something demons like Veishti could feed off for years."

It wasn't fair. Veishti hadn't been concerned with keeping the humans in any kind of emotional check, so Rakmanon wasn't making any sense. They'd succeeded in defeating the fear demon, and now Archie was free from his sentence of death. Wasn't that worth something?

Rakmanon bunched his fist. "You haven't saved anyone, you know. Veishti will need to recover, and he'll do that by taking other victims. He'll have to."

He paced up and down, and for a moment she thought he was going to kick her. From the ground, she had a very good view of his feet - with three large toes and a dew claw, they were proper demonic feet, strong and distinctive. So unlike her own pale, little, human-style ones.

He hadn't finished. "I can see I've been too indulgent with you. From now on, you're not to poison any demons unless I tell you to. And stay away from Veishti and his thralls. Now go, get out of my sight! I don't know if I can stand to look at you any longer."

She backed away on her knees, only rising to run away when she was out of range. The door slammed shut behind her, swiftly followed by the crash of broken pottery. She felt drained, emotionally and . . . physically.

CHAPTER 7

It didn't make sense. Rakmanon had been so happy for them, so proud of her, after the convocation. And now this dressing-down? What was up with her master?

Kenssie considered her options. He hadn't forbidden her to see Permilia, and Archie wasn't one of Veishti's thralls any more.

Half an hour later, she swung into Permilia's drive in the Mercedes and killed the engine. Voices rose in argument from the house, Permilia's high and screechy and Archie's deep and intense. Under them, the drone of the TV news. Now that she wasn't preparing for a battle, she noticed the weeds growing in the angle between the pavement and the house, and the way the front of the letterbox was missing. In the corridor, she ran her finger along the dado rail and flicked inches of dust off the peeling paintwork.

"You're not doing it. Not after everything I've been through to get you out."

Archie wasn't backing down. "I am. I have to."

Kenssie found the two of them in the kitchen. Permilia was red-faced and radiating upset.

"Hi," Kenssie said.

Permilia spared her a glance and returned her attention to her son.

"He wants to be a thrall. Can you believe it?"

Archie's jaw was set.

"Veishti's thrall?" she asked.

Archie gave her a withering look. "No, dumbass. I want to be the thrall of someone who can protect me from demons like him."

"That's not how thralldom works," Permilia said. "Tell him, Kenssie."

Kenssie shrugged. "Apparently I'm a dumbass. You think he'll listen to me?"

Archie scowled and folded his arms. From a certain angle, he looked a lot like a stroppy human teenager, but the horns told another story. He was probably closer to eighty.

"This is serious," Permilia said, turning back to him. "I don't want you throwing your future away. You're three-quarters; you don't have to be anyone's thrall."

So much came down to blood. If Archie had that much demonic blood, that meant his father had to be almost a pure-bred demon. Whoever he was.

"Name me one master demon who's three-quarters," Archie challenged.

Permilia pursed her lips and said nothing.

"You can't. They're all fullblood. The sooner I find a suitable replacement, the safer I'll be from him."

Archie started to stride out the room.

"Stop!" Permilia screeched. "Stop!"

Archie turned.

Permilia's tone was desperate. "At least think about what I've said. Don't do this."

He gave his mother his most acid look yet. "Relax, I'm not going to do it right now. I just need some space from you. I'm going to my room."

Permilia sighed. "Good. Well, you can have my room. You'll be safer in there, it's lead-lined."

"Lead-lined?" Kenssie mouthed when he was out of sight. "That doesn't work."

"Did your master tell you that? I'm sure he'd like you to think it. It works some; I've had experience."

Kenssie could well imagine it. Permilia seemed to make it her business to defy not just her own master but everyone else's. She was some kind of thrall liberation revolutionary. What drove her?

"Who is yours?" she asked the witch.

Permilia paused as if she was debating whether to tell. As though saying the name had power.

"Salamhat."

The black demon. She didn't know what his hunger was, but she remembered his derisive laughter. He was the one who had suggested the test, if that thing with Inkado had really been a test at all. She owed him payback.

"You know why I'm here. Tell me about the book."

"Don't forget it's a grimoire," Permilia said. "Magical mojos."

Kenssie snorted in derision. "As if. Just tell me where I can find it."

The witch did, in detail and with maps. When she was done, she flicked the kettle on and started arranging mugs.

"So, are we going to do this thing?" Kenssie asked.

"We? You know I can't come with you."

Kenssie didn't know that.

"What!? After all the help I've given you!"

"Salamhat's forbidden it."

Kenssie narrowed her eyes. "What does he know about this?"

"Nothing. He forbade me years ago to steal or interfere with the council's sacred objects. I'm not allowed to reveal their location to pureblood demons or witches either. But since you're not strictly one or the other . . ."

Kenssie frowned at the dig.

"What use is this knowledge if I've got to go in with no backup? If I get caught, they'll strip my powers and chuck me in a pit."

"These are the guys who make the laws, remember. The penalty is death."

"All the more reason to have a helper. Can't you do anything?"

Permilia shook her head regretfully. Kenssie chewed her lip. It seemed like the witch had backed her into this situation because she couldn't do it for herself, and Kenssie hadn't so much won a concession from her as gained another job. A job she was eager to carry out, but not recklessly. Her gaze went to the second door, and upwards to where the lead-lined bedroom would be.

Permilia jumped to the door and spread both arms across it. "Oh, no, you don't! Not a chance. Not when he's unthralled and vulnerable."

"Vulnerable? You've changed your tone. He's not under anyone's direction; he'll be a free agent. That could come in handy."

"Kenssie, he's my son. Maybe you don't know how that feels, but one day you will. Don't say anything to him, I'm begging you. You must have other friends you can ask."

Kenssie rolled her shoulders back and raised her chin. "You're right, of course I do. What was I thinking?"

She scooped up the maps and turned on her heel.

***

She flicked through map screens on her mobile. This was surely the place. It radiated the kind of just-like-any-other-place-ness that only occurred when a location was trying too hard to blend in. She'd driven past it a couple of times, and if that wasn't a sure sign of a psychic block, she didn't know what was.

"Meet the new mayor of Pwning the Demon Council; population: one."

She'd come alone. Of the four entries in her address book, one of them was Rakmanon - who couldn't know about this - one was living in Russia, and the other two lived in Wales and thought she ran her own gym and commanded a team of six thralls.

Birds in the trees stopped tweeting, spooked by her disembodied voice. The copse was full of tall beech and oak, and evenly green. No tell-tale bare patches to indicate untrodden areas, no scorch marks from recent fires, nothing at all out of the ordinary. If anything, the place was too green, given that it hadn't rained in a fortnight.

She picked her way through bracken and crackly twigs until she came to a thick, well-rotted log lying across the way. She shoved her hand into it up to her elbow and felt amongst the leaf mould and earwigs. When her fingers found the keypad, she knew she was in the right place. Nine buttons, like a telephone pad.

1-4-7-8-9-6-3-2. Kenssie keyed the numbers in, following them round the pad like a square. For a moment she held her breath, wondering if she really ought to duck and roll to avoid poison darts. Nothing. Then a click and a whirr, and her heart leapt.

On the other side of the log a rectangular section of ground dipped and slid downwards and sideways, revealing a steel staircase.

"Too much Indiana, girl," she told herself. "No-one really does that stuff."

Nevertheless she couldn't help looking sideways at the trees in case they erupted with flying blades or the like.

She took a deep breath of fresh, earthy air before stepping

cautiously down into the concealed tunnel. Her boots clanged noisily on the steps, but she reminded herself it didn't matter. There was no-one to hear. At the bottom the tunnel stretched into darkness, and she wondered at the wisdom of bringing only one torch. She had a mobile phone, but the light from that wouldn't last.

On the wall beside her was another keypad. She keyed in the numbers - in reverse this time. Above her the mechanism whirred smoothly again, blocking out the daylight. She ran up the steps, but the last sliver of light closed off and she had to pull her fingers out of the gap so they didn't get crushed by the heavy door. She was plunged into blackness.

"Knickers!"

Then the lights flickered on, and she could see clearly. The tunnel was square and reminded her of an old mine shaft, except its walls were concrete like a bomb shelter. It could well have been purpose-built by the council. Permilia had warned her of booby traps. But it would be okay so long as she knew the codes to disarm them. The council intended to be able to reach their grimoire themselves, so it couldn't be impossible to get to.

The corridor was about eighty metres long and paved with red and white tiles in a chessboard pattern. Kenssie's footsteps rang out as she stepped forwards.

The first trap was at a panel that looked like an electrical utility board. She opened the plastic cover and found eight thick switches in the "off" position. Apparently this was a ruse, and they needed to be "on" to disarm the device. Briefly Kenssie wondered whether Permilia was trying to get rid of her. But of course not, it was too elaborate. She flipped all the switches, looked up, and hoped. Breathed in. If she was wrong, slicing blades would fall from the ceiling and turn her into sandwich ham.

"Welcome, Councillor," buzzed the voice from the machine. "Intruder repellent number one is disarmed."

Kenssie exhaled. Two to go. She stepped on gingerly, noting the fat Damoclean blades that glinted hungrily from the ceiling.

Next up there was a second panel, this one disguised as a gas meter. Not very imaginative, these demons. That had to be a good thing. She ran her fingers down the side of the unit, looking for the hidden catch, and opened the front pane. Then she turned the dials on the meter to the number Permilia had given her. Once again she held her breath. Her eyes darted up anxiously. She didn't even know what this one did if it were sprung.

"Intruder repellent two is disarmed."

The smooth female voice sounded kinda smug. Or was that her paranoia talking? Her boots clicked as she walked towards the last obstacle. It was a safe, and the combination was the final security measure. She had precisely one chance to get it right, or the alarm would sound and she'd be locked in.

The safe was a big metal box about head height, its base welded to the floor. It had a mechanical dial on the front with a red logo in the centre, the broken circle with a dot in the middle that was the sign of the council. She pressed the logo and stepped back.

A blue and white hologram flickered to life, projected about an inch from the front of the safe. Fiuru's image, glaring crossly to the side. Then she looked directly at Kenssie and her face settled into a plastic smile. Her lips moved silently. Then sound came out of a small speaker on the safe somewhere, out of sync with the image. Fiuru's hologram paused to smirk.

"If you're here, it's because you're either a council member or a very lucky intruder. Either way, you'd better know the answer to my question: what is the most beautiful number? You have thirty seconds."

The projection changed to a big, fat ten-button keypad, but instead of alphanumeric keys there were symbols in their place. Above this, a countdown that moved from thirty to twenty-nine. As it did so, all the symbols on the keypad changed.

The most beautiful number? Was she talking about Pi, the galactic constant, the golden mean? It didn't matter; Kenssie couldn't remember any of them past a few digits. She screwed her eyes up, and tried to concentrate. Twenty-eight seconds left.

Permilia had said it wasn't a riddle. "The numbers are right in front of you. It's a test of dexterity and intelligence."

Well, that was her stuffed and served with mushrooms. When the display changed to twenty-seven she realised it was taking much longer than a second - maybe three seconds each time. So what was she supposed to believe, the time on the display or that on the audio? Panic rose. She didn't know what to do; something horrible was going to happen to her and she couldn't stop it. She couldn't even escape the tunnel because it was locked behind her.

Think, Kenssie. You muppet.

Twenty-six. Twenty-five.

The number's right in front of you.

The only numbers in front of her were the seconds ticking away. She decided to try those, but where did she put them? All the symbols kept changing. She imagined the display as a telephone pad and pressed the hologram buttons where three and zero would normally be.

Bing! Bing!

The ringing noise seemed encouraging. She pressed two and nine, poking her finger into the air, and so on down the rest of the countdown. Somehow the contraption picked up on her movements and she was rewarded by a series of rings. Then she got to nineteen and accidentally trailed her hand across two buttons at once.

There was an angry buzz.

"Start again," the unit instructed.

She breathed in. She could do this.

30-29-28-27

Point. Breathe. Point. Breathe. Try not to shake.

With one "second" on the countdown she poked the final zero, her whole body tense. She'd done her best, now the chips would fall. What was it going to be - poison gas, slicing blades, a furnace? She screwed her eyes half-closed, barely daring to look.

"Welcome, Councillor," the recording said.

The hologram fell away and the dial turned. Something clicked inside the safe, and the thick steel door opened. This was it. She'd done it! Now she was going to find out what gave the council all their power over lesser demons. Find out, and use it against them.

She felt a buzzing energy from the grimoire as soon as the safe was opened. The safe had to be lead-lined, because the feeling hit her like a tsunami of life and emotion. It fair crackled. The book was hefty, bound in what looked like human skin, mid-brown and stitched finely along its edges. There was no title.

She reached in and touched it. A static surge of power pulsed up her arm. This was the real deal all right; the spellbook felt alive.

"Come to mama," she said.

It had to be filled with juicy, delicious spells if it felt this good to touch. It felt as heavy and solid as a brick, and it smelt of new leather. She opened it reverentially.

"Huh?"

The first page was blank. Well, it hardly needed a copyright notice. The second page was also blank. And the next. She leafed through, finding nothing but empty pages, finally flicking them past like a primitive moving picture book. The heavy white paper was entirely blank. She turned the book spine upwards and shook it. Nothing came out.

"Put that down!"

Salamhat's voice boomed from the other end of the corridor. She spun, tucking the grimoire behind her back. Salamhat was with a few of his thralls, and Fiuru followed him down the steps. One of the thralls with them was Permilia. Of course. Kenssie hadn't thrown the alarm, so how else would they know to come here just in time to catch her at this?

Her nails dug into the grimoire, and it sent a surge of raw energy through her, a jolt of elation. If this was the last chance she'd get to hold the book, then she was going to grip it tight.

"Let go of the grimoire!" Salamhat commanded.

"How dare you touch it!" Fiuru yelled. "How dare you come here, thrall!"

Kenssie said nothing. If experience had taught her anything, it was that pleading with these demons was a waste of breath.

"Seize her," Salamhat told his thralls. They poured down the stairs after him, a sea of smaller demons accompanied by some of Fiuru's grey contingent.

Kenssie offered no resistance as they swarmed her and wrestled the book away. She tried to look as it went back in the safe, but arms were shoving and pushing her down the corridor, back the way she came. She was brought before Salamhat and Fiuru with her arms in the firm grip of several thralls.

"Have you got anything to say for yourself, you pathetic herbivore?" Fiuru demanded.

Permilia was behind her master, trying to catch Kenssie's eye. Kenssie knew she was trying to apologise, to excuse what she'd done, and it wouldn't wash. She refused to meet the witch's gaze.

"Ignorant animal," Fiuru said, slapping her across the cheek.

CHAPTER 8

Thick, succulent vines held fast to Kenssie's arms and legs, and wrapped around her whole body. They twisted round her horns, poked her earlobes, tickled her eyes, and even tried to explore her mouth - until she bit down hard on one. She was pinned in a star shape to the dank dungeon wall by a mobile plant. It grew up from a large, earthy rectangle on the ground. In theory, that meant she could dig her way out of the dungeon given time, but the local flora wasn't letting her move an inch.

For something to do, she tried to move her limbs. The vines tightened around her. They squeezed her chest and neck until she couldn't breathe, and this made Kenssie panic. She had to fight it, if only to get enough space to inhale, but the more she moved the more the vines constricted her. She was choking, her face turning blue.

"Don't do that."

The voice came from close by, but she couldn't see anyone. There was a single, bare, energy-saving bulb lighting the corridor outside, which was visible through a barred window in the upper half of the door. It threw everything in the cell into harsh relief or deep shadow.

"Un-un?" she replied when she got her breath.

The voice was irate. "Keep still. Tamzeli likes you to struggle."

"Who's that?"

"I'm Netammu. I'm right beside you. I'd reach out to show you how close, but . . . you know."

She couldn't turn her head, but through the corner of her eye she noticed the plant was bulkier down to her left.

"How did you offend the council?"

"I didn't. Sometimes Tamzeli reaches out and grabs one of us as well."

"You don't sound too worried."

"I'll get out as soon as Fiuru remembers I'm gone."

"You're Fiuru's thrall? You poor sod."

"Says the demoness in her dungeon. Cow face."

"I beg your pardon?"

"I said cow face. With a side order of slack-jawed custard-drooling mush-muncher."

"There's no need to be rude."

"Sorry. Standing orders to offend everyone I see. No offence."

"Don't you think she'll come and pull you out a lot quicker if you don't do your job to the best of your ability?"

"Point."

They hung in silence for a while, listening to the drip-drip of water on a nearby stone. The cool, dark cell encouraged the contemplation of things done and not done. The Tamzeli held her like an all-over corset with firm, smooth vines the width of her arm. Its deep green surface was textured with fine, soft hairs. Her breathing returned to normal and misted lightly in front of her.

How had it come to this? And what would they do to her?

Deep down, she knew the unpalatable answer to the first. Permilia had betrayed her. The witch had been right there next to her master when they'd come for her, and it didn't seem likely he had just happened to be in the area when she was stealing the grimoire. Permilia had set this all up. It had been her idea all along, and the witch could have been in collusion with her masters every step of the way in an elaborate scheme to discredit her. And now here she was, completely in their power, guilty of breaking into their vault when all she'd wanted to do was get back what they'd wrongfully taken from her in the first place. They'd use it as an excuse to punish her. Her stomach clutched as she thought about how that would go: execution, or imprisonment?

The Tamzeli squeezed her tighter.

Netammu interrupted her train of thought. "It's your own fault you're here."

"What would you know about it?"

"Apart from being there when you were arrested, you mean?

That's got to be the most botched break-in I've seen in a thousand years."

"It was going all right until someone grassed me up."

"You didn't even have backup. Amateur."

"It was n- oh."

Belatedly she realised what his game was.

"I forgive you," she said. "I know you can't help it."

"I'm trying to divert your despair. Idiot."

"You know, for one of the Wasp's minions you're actually not too bad."

"Thanks."

"If we weren't stuck in this dungeon, maybe we'd hang out - you know, socially."

"We are hanging out."

Kenssie smiled. She might be stuck in a dank hole, but there was no way she'd give the council her anger or her despair so easily. They'd have to come and wrest those feelings out of her.

As if on cue, footsteps rang down the corridor. The door opened, briefly making her eyeballs ache with the increasing light. Fiuru and Haames stood silhouetted in the doorway. Haames's tentacles were as mobile as ever, like hair agitated by too much static.

"Come to take me out so soon?" Kenssie asked. "I'm having such fun."

"She's got a mouth on her," Haames said to Fiuru.

"I can fix that," Fiuru said with a nasty grin. She stepped closer.

Kenssie thought about asking what they intended to do to her, but stopped herself. That would be playing into their hands. It didn't matter how scared she really felt, or how angry. The important thing was to appear unaffected.

Fiuru's smile dropped when she realised her threat wasn't having the intended effect. Her wide mouth dissolved into a pout. Strong, offensive perfume clogged the air in a cloud around her. She leaned in, and Kenssie noticed how her upswept horns curved elegantly inwards in delicately twisted spirals to a point over her high-cheekboned, totally symmetrical face. Kenssie couldn't understand why she'd be so keen to evolve herself into something else, but perhaps a thousand-year perspective made you look at the world in a different way.

"Are you bored with your face?" Kenssie asked her.

Fiuru ignored the question. "Perhaps you don't realise the gravity of your situation. You took council property. Sacred council property. Normally the penalty for that is death."

Fiuru stepped around the cell, her cloven heels grating on grimy flagstones.

"You do know your sacred book is empty," Kenssie said.

Fiuru spun round and growled. "Empty? Is that what you think? Stupider and stupider. It's you who can't read it, witchblood."

Haames shook his tentacles at her, and Fiuru joined in with a cawing laugh.

"Tell her the deal," Haames said.

"Oh, yes, this is your situation. Many at the council wanted to see you executed, but I convinced them otherwise. So you owe me a debt. You will become my thrall."

Kenssie's face fell. She couldn't help it. She couldn't lose Rakmanon! The thought of it paralysed her. Her limbs stiffened and she tried to clench her fists. The Tamzeli squeezed air out of her lungs.

Her reply was whispered. "I'm Rakmanon's thrall. You have no right to deprive him."

"We have every right," Fiuru said loudly.

"So my choice is death or re-enthralment?"

"Oh, no, there's no choice," Fiuru said. "The decision has already been made."

Fiuru adopted a cocky grin. Kenssie met her yellow eyes and tried to make herself calm down. It wasn't hard for her to imagine this demon taking her from her master – she had a talent for making anyone angry.

A shiver of power travelled up her spine. For a flash she felt the same way she had when she'd touched the grimoire for the first time. Then it was gone, but it left her with an idea.

"Go on, then, if you're going to do it," she told Fiuru. "Get it over with."

Fiuru wagged her finger. "No, no, no, no, no. We'll do this properly, tomorrow in the council chamber. I just wanted to tell you in advance so you'll have time to get used to the idea."

Time to stew over it, more like. The demoness was so transparent.

Fiuru turned on her heel and sashayed out. There was a muffled grunt from Netammu as he struggled to make himself heard.

Somehow he'd got a vine lodged in his face. Fiuru turned to regard her minion.

"Tamzeli, release . . . no, on second thoughts, don't release Netammu yet. He's been negligent in his duties and I want him punished."

The demons left, slamming the door with a heavy finality. Haames flicked out a tentacle as he left the corridor and flipped off the light, plunging them into darkness as a final insult.

CHAPTER 9

Kenssie rubbed her arms. The Tamzeli plant had left pressure marks, and although she bounced back from such hurts very quickly the memory left her feeling vulnerable. It wasn't the right frame of mind to face the council in. Her hands and feet were shackled in lead irons. A thrall prodded her from behind and she stumbled forwards into the chamber. It was brightly lit, or perhaps it seemed more glaring because she'd become used to the dungeon's dimness.

The gallery above was empty. Then, bit by bit, the council members walked in, chatting merrily amongst themselves and making her feel like a cardboard display. They were relaxed, as though this were a social gathering. She inhaled slowly and tried to feel nothing: strong emotions would play into their hands.

All of the faces she scanned were of councillors or their thralls. It didn't seem to be a public meeting. Where was Rakmanon? She may have disgraced herself, but she'd give anything to see him - or even Jenny - at this moment. Was he too angry with her to come? Did he even know what was about to happen?

Haames stood and drew the court to quivering order.

"Welcome, councillors. The prisoner you see before you is Kenssie, thrall of Rakmanon. She is guilty of trespass and the attempted theft of council property. In your mercy and wisdom you have agreed to commute her sentence of death to one of compulsory re-enthralment."

Kenssie smirked. "Mercy and wisdom? It's called greed."

"Be silent in court!" Haames yelled.

"Make me."

"We're about to," Fiuru said.

Kenssie met her jaundice-yellow eyes. Fiuru was dressed in sober black, but she wore a thick necklace of blood diamonds and a smile as wide as a lottery winner's. But whatever Fiuru thought, Kenssie wasn't about to make it easy for the higher demon. She smiled sweetly.

"You have a high opinion of yourself, for someone who looks like a liver-damaged mortal."

Fiuru's smile didn't move, but the skin round her eyes twitched once. Haames clapped his tentacles together.

"Fiuru, if you please. You may proceed."

The yellow peril stepped up to the podium at the front of the gallery. The sound of fidgeting and rustling papers hushed, and the audience of demons leaned in for a better view. It was now or never, Kenssie realised. Fiuru was going to pull her free of her master, and she'd lose him from her life. She'd lose a lot more than that if the state of Fiuru's thralls was anything to go by - her tongue, at the very least.

Kenssie gathered her strength, and focused her will on the demoness. A surge of power ran through her, making her fingers tingle as she pushed it outwards. The air shimmered, and then the vision hit Kenssie with such high definition she thought for a moment she'd left the courtroom. But no - she could still feel the irons. She was simply seeing and hearing Fiuru's memory almost as though she were living through it, like a ghost hitching a ride in someone else's consciousness.

She saw a well-appointed drawing room with a tall window looking out over acres of lawn. A demon stood next to it, a young male dressed in Georgian style. The tilt of his head suggested he was a household servant. He had a light green complexion and four short horns, and when he raised his head to look at her she could see he had a pleasant oval face and sad eyes.

"Mistress." His voice was soft, musical.

Fiuru's voice was unchanged, although this was clearly a different century. "I have a document for you."

She handed him a folded letter, sealed with wax. He took it with a question in his eyes.

"Don't open it yet. First, listen to what I have to tell you. This is a very special time for you, and I've chosen you for this privilege because you're . . . my favourite."

She paused to assess his reaction. He looked curious rather than pleased.

She went on. "And, because you're my favourite, I think it's time for you to evolve. That's the design, which you will follow to the best of your ability."

The air went thick with the smog of demonic influence. It was a command he would be bound to obey.

"In two weeks," she continued, "you will begin your evolution. Your new form will be greater, stronger, and more specialised than you've ever been. You will have to lose a few features you've grown used to, of course. But when you've made the change you'll agree you'll be something better than you've ever been. None will compare to you."

The servant bowed his head. "As you wish, mistress."

His attitude was submissive, and he hadn't lost the sadness in his eyes. Fiuru stepped closer and reached out with an elegant golden arm decorated with pale blue sapphires. She put her hand under his chin and tilted his head up. Kenssie could feel the frustration arcing between them.

"I have great plans for you, Tamzeli."

Abruptly Kenssie was back in the courtroom, looking up at the eager faces of councillors, leaning over like Romans watching lions eat Christians. Her mouth fell open as she looked at Fiuru, whose brow was furrowed in concentration.

"You turned him into a plant!"

"What?" Fiuru looked confused, but she recovered quickly. "I had every right. He's my thrall, my property."

Murmurs went round the room.

"How did she know that?" Suninn asked.

"Lucky guess," said Salamhat.

Kenssie felt anger bubble up at the injustice of it. She wanted to reach up and smack Fiuru for her cruelty. She'd taken Tamzeli for a plant, but he was a demon and a thrall like she was, and Fiuru had turned him into a monster and hidden him away in a dungeon for eternity. She clenched her fists. She couldn't hurt Fiuru physically, her thralls would see to that, but she was so mad. Fiuru's eyes were lighting up with power as she fed off Kenssie's rage.

Don't get mad, get even.

"It's no guess. I read it straight from Fiuru's mind."

Collective intakes of breath went round the room.

"Pathetic lie," Fiuru countered.

Kenssie pointed at the demoness, her heavy manacles making it an effort. "You did it because he was in love with another, and you were jealous."

The demons in the gallery looked at each other, their mouths dropping open.

"Ha, ha, ha, ha," Fiuru said, utterly failing to make a realistic imitation of a laugh.

What Kenssie had suggested was not only taboo, it was highly embarrassing for Fiuru. Demon masters were supposed to have full control over their thralls, so if Fiuru wanted Tamzeli to love her, all she had to do was tell him to. Yet Kenssie knew she'd spoken the truth: Fiuru couldn't make her thrall obey her in this instance. What she couldn't work out was why.

Kenssie was drawn into other visions, only this time they weren't ones she had control over. Puppies getting run over. Stupid humans chopping down redwoods and dumping nuclear waste in the sea. Whales getting harpooned. Kenssie was kneeling, although she didn't remember getting down, and before her there was a small thrall manacled to the wall. It was Netammu.

Fiuru walked onto the scene dressed in high heels and shiny black leathers, and holding a long, barbed whip. She cracked it in the air once to test it. Satisfied with it, she smiled, and then turned to her thrall. Netammu had bitten his lip until it bled and he was wincing. Tears tracked down his chubby grey face.

On the ground lay a sword, its grey steel dull against the concrete floor. Kenssie's own manacles clinked when she moved, drawing attention, but for now Fiuru's concentration was elsewhere. Kenssie could reach the weapon, but she'd only get one shot to wield it. Fiuru raised her arm to strike her defenceless thrall. If Kenssie took the sword she'd be lost, but she couldn't let Fiuru get away with this.

"Stop this now!"

Rakmanon's voice boomed rich and deep, and the scene dissolved. Her master entered, a towering red presence in crotch-cut green flares and matching biker jacket, slit for his wings. He came to stand by her, elbowing the thralls out of his way. He seemed to take up most of the courtroom.

"Release her," he told the thralls.

They didn't move, deferring to Fiuru.

"Ah, Rakmanon, so nice to see you," Fiuru said. "You should be here to witness this."

"You have no right to her."

"I had it under control," Kenssie muttered. Rakmanon noticed, of course, and gave her his I'll-deal-with-you-later eyebrow, then turned back to the Queen Hornet.

"Wrong," Fiuru said. "You forfeited your rights when you let her try to steal our property."

"Do you mean this?"

Rakmanon pulled the book from his jacket and held it aloft. His wings extended as he did so, an assertion of a challenge. The gallery erupted in whispers. He stood waiting for hush to descend. It didn't.

"How dare you!" Salamhat yelled from the back.

This was dangerous; the anger in the room was palpable, and it could tip the balance in Fiuru's favour. But Rakmanon simply stood his ground and let a sly grin curl up his face.

"You forget to whom you are speaking, Salamhat. Maybe one day I'll teach you how I dare."

Rakmanon flipped open the pages. Slowly he showed them to the audience, blank leaf after blank leaf.

"It's a copy," Suninn said.

Rakmanon turned another page.

"You're not powerful enough to read it," Salamhat said.

Another page rustled over.

"He's casting a vision," Fiuru said.

"Over all of us? He's not that strong," Haames said.

Rakmanon's reply rose over all of them. "This is your power? Your secret? Your holy of holies? Frankly, I've seen better in Poundland."

It was the real book. Kenssie could feel its power thickening the air from where she was standing. It was drawing something out of the room. She inched closer, hoping to touch it. But Rakmanon closed the grimoire with a snap and tucked it into his jacket.

"That's ours!" Fiuru yelled.

Rakmanon wagged a finger. "Now, now, you know the rules. A thrall belongs to whoever can keep him."

He reached across to Kenssie and touched her manacles with the tip of his finger. The metal cracked where he pointed, and the bonds fell to the ground.

CHAPTER 10

They were back in Rakmanon's office block. The large windows were open where they'd flown in. She pulled them shut, blocking out the noises of the blustery wind and the city. For the moment they were alone, just her and her master. And the book. Rakmanon's mouth was a downturned slash of disapproval, but she'd take that over Fiuru's malicious grin any day. In fact, she wanted to kiss him. He had, after all, come to her rescue.

"What just happened?" she asked.

"I should be asking you that. You disappear for days, and then I get word you're on trial and Fiuru's about to take you forcibly from me. What were you thinking?"

"I took a secret right from Fiuru's head. From a higher demon!"

"You what?"

"Tamzeli. She didn't want the council to know what she'd done to him, or why. She fed off his anger, so she wasn't strong enough to make him love her and to keep him as her thrall at the same time. So she made him a monster."

Rakmanon puffed his chest up and lifted his chin so that he looked down his nose at her even more than usual.

"I thought you learned that from her thralls."

"Nope, I pulled it right out of her."

She grinned. She could still feel the energy of that secret coursing through her, giving her strength. Maybe now he would treat her with more respect - less as a subordinate, more as a partner? She'd earned it.

"Kenssie, I forbid you to use your power to draw secrets from my mind."

Her temples throbbed with the force of his command. It hadn't even crossed her mind to do so, but now she couldn't help but wonder what he had to hide.

"While you're at it, you could forbid me to fly faster than light, or to crochet tea cosies whilst watching TV talent shows about country music."

"It's for your own good."

"Oh, yeah? How?"

Kenssie pictured him keeping his secret passion for her hidden, perhaps writing squishy poems about it in a diary he tucked under the floorboards, being too ashamed of his feelings to express them fully. Then she took a look at his glossy, bright green outfit, with the jacket flapping open to reveal every inch of his six-pack. Or was it an eight-pack? She didn't want to stare, but his torso seemed to go on forever. Shame? That wasn't his style at all.

"Well," he said, breaking up her contemplation of his abs. "For one thing, you don't want to know where I'll be hiding this."

He drew the grimoire out of his jacket. She moved closer.

"Go on, then, you can touch it."

She put her hand on the skin binding, and its familiar rush coursed through her.

"I don't understand. How is it that a grimoire with no spells means so much to them?"

"It's a symbol," he said.

"Just a symbol?"

"Is there such a thing as just a symbol?"

"It's a thrall as well, isn't it? I can feel it's alive."

"It is."

"Can it be changed back?"

Rakmanon stroked his chin. "I don't know. It may never have looked anything like you or I."

She stroked her thumb across its surface, feeling it purr with energy. It was hard to believe such a small object was of any import. Its skin was fine-grained, even a little sticky.

Rakmanon snatched it back.

"Stop that. You're probably rubbing its bum."

Kenssie flushed. As usual, he had an unerring knack for what not to say. She folded her arms and scowled.

"Right," he said, remembering he was displeased with her. "I'm tempted to lock you in a cupboard somewhere so you can't get into more trouble. But your disobedience has left me hungry. Get out there and harvest me some humiliation."

"Rak, I'm sorry."

"Huh," he snorted.

"Thanks for saving me from Fiuru."

She wanted to show him she meant it, so she stepped up to give him a hug. He stepped back and waved her away before she made contact.

"Go on, get on with it. You've work to do."

Shamefaced, she backed out of his office. She wondered briefly whether he had been feeding from her and leaving her weak. But the idea was absurd, so she dismissed it with a shake of her head. He would never do that to her.

Jenny was in the corridor, balancing an overfull mug of tea. She'd installed a kettle and all this human food paraphernalia to go with it, as well as a geranium. Its strong, peppery scent didn't quite mask all the rest of the smells. It would present a convincing front to any curious mortals who happened to be spying on their offices, but she didn't know how Rakmanon was putting up with it.

The witch sat down and stared at a piece of paper, not meeting her eyes. Well, Kenssie wasn't going to let that pass; she'd had enough of other people's rudeness for one day. She reached across and took the page out of Jenny's hand.

"Ah!"

Jenny jumped and splashed hot tea on her arm. She put a hand to her chest.

"Rakmanon, don't do that! You took me by surprise."

Jenny recovered her breath and dabbed at the spill with a tissue. The witch wasn't snubbing her; she really couldn't see her at all. With an effort she concentrated, and dropped her demonic veil. Jenny's eye whites showed.

"Kenssie! You're back! And you've got your invisibility! Oh, heck, this is going to be fun."

Kenssie grinned. "Oh, yes, I'm back."

Jenny sorted through the papers piled on her desk.

"This came for you."

She handed Kenssie an envelope containing a handwritten note in flowing, beautifully looped script.

"It was from a witch with a big Rasta hat. I think she had horns."

"Thanks."

She read the first part.

Dear Kenssie,

I'm so sorry about all you've endured, but believe me I didn't intend things to turn out this way. Meet me at . . .

The witch leant over and angled her head to peer at the text.

"Is it anything interesting?" Jenny asked.

Kenssie crumpled the letter and pinged it into the wastepaper bin.

"Nothing important. Be seeing you, Jenny."

Kenssie winked out of the witch's vision and strolled to the lift. She had mischief to attend to.

THE END

Kenssie's story continues with

DIABOLICAL TASTE

ABOUT THE AUTHOR

Rock singer, xenobiologist and ninja are just some of the jobs Ros wishes she could put on her CV. She has blogged about books at warpcoresf.co.uk for over a decade, and has done a wide range of different jobs whilst dreaming of the written word. She lives in Lincolnshire under the iron rule of a grumpy black cat.

www.ingramcontent.com/pod-product-compliance
Lightning Source LLC
Chambersburg PA
CBHW030539180626
46810CB00005B/1940